"You don't have to [...] minute."

Candy shrugged. He might be right, but he also might be wrong. She hadn't received any other assignment. "You're my detail."

He grimaced. "I didn't want that. If I'd wanted a full-time assistant, I'd have brought one along. I'm sure you have a whole bunch of things to do that are more important than shepherding me around."

Candy felt a flicker of amusement. "I understand why you might not want that. But I'm equally certain the city fathers didn't toss this to the sheriff because they wanted you rolling through here like a loose cannon. I guess I'm the city protection squad. No bad publicity here."

That drew a grin from him. "You might be right. Most of the places I've been to have been too big to worry about it. Not only is Conard City way smaller, but it's also pretty isolated."

"Yup. They'd like to draw more visitors, not drive them away. So please, Steve, make us look good."

CONARD COUNTY: HARD PROOF

New York Times Bestselling Author

Rachel Lee

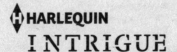

HARLEQUIN
INTRIGUE

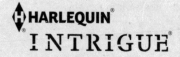

HARLEQUIN®
INTRIGUE®

ISBN-13: 978-1-335-13669-5

Conard County: Hard Proof

Copyright © 2020 by Susan Civil-Brown

Recycling programs
for this product may
not exist in your area.

For questions and comments about the quality of this book,
please contact us at CustomerService@Harlequin.com.

Harlequin Enterprises ULC
22 Adelaide St. West, 40th Floor
Toronto, Ontario M5H 4E3, Canada
www.Harlequin.com

Printed in U.S.A.

Rachel Lee was hooked on writing by the age of twelve and practiced her craft as she moved from place to place all over the United States. This *New York Times* bestselling author now resides in Florida and has the joy of writing full-time.

Visit the Author Profile page at Harlequin.com.

CAST OF CHARACTERS

Candela (Candy) Serrano—Conard County sheriff's deputy, combat veteran. Assigned as liaison to *Ghostly Ties* program.

Steve Hawks—Former big-city detective, now host of the TV program *Ghostly Ties*. A strong skeptic.

The Castelle family—Annabelle and Todd and their seven-year-old daughter, Vivian. Viv hears voices in her bedroom and is terrified.

Ben Wittes—Local psychic who comes to help with Steve's program.

Chapter One

Steve Hawks glanced impatiently at his watch. Time was getting on, Conard City was nowhere in view and he had an appointment to keep. He hated being late.

If it hadn't been for the obstacle in the road that had been too small to see, he wouldn't be this far behind. Damn tire change. At least the rental company had provided a full-size tire, not a doughnut, which would have slowed him even more.

Ah, well, he could try his cell again, if he could get a signal out here. Looking at the open expanse with mountains in the distance, he doubted he would.

Oh, hell. For once the world would have to wait for him.

He had a couple of weeks before his production crew arrived, but it was necessary to do groundwork for his TV show: *Ghostly Ties*. He had to know his clients, had to know the area and fill in some local history before filming.

Although he'd been at it for three years now, Steve sometimes found it difficult to say he hosted "one of those ghostie shows." A far cry from his former life as a detective. However, he figured it was just a different type of investigation. He looked for rational explanations and he delighted in local history and lore. All of which required a lot of detective work.

Quit it, he told himself. He didn't mind the work at all. In fact, he enjoyed it. Without it, he couldn't have sent his parents to a happy retirement in Costa Rica. Great side benefit.

So he drove down this aging state highway, amid ranches—was that what they were called or were these something else?—looking at endless square miles of browning autumn grasses and trees. And occasionally a bunch of cows. Or steers.

He laughed at himself. He had a lot to learn out here.

Then he saw a large flock of sheep. Okay, was that a *sheep* ranch? He shook his head and hoped he didn't make a total fool out of himself before he could ask the right questions. Not that it really mattered. He'd realized long ago that you made more friends if you could laugh at yourself.

At long last, he saw what appeared to be rectangular shapes rising in the distance. It sure wasn't the slowly rolling hills he'd been seeing most of the way. At least the mountains appeared to be growing. For the longest time, the mountains hadn't seemed to be coming closer. Now they did. Big and looming.

And that must be Conard City up ahead. A huge semi and trailer seemed to come out of nowhere over the lip of a rise and roared past him, buffeting his car a bit. So there *was* life out here.

He'd been to many places in his life, but he honestly couldn't remember one with such huge empty expanses.

DEPUTY CANDELA SERRANO, Candy for short, waited in the sheriff's office for the arrival of Steve Hawks. She'd drawn the "short straw" for who was going to babysit the guy, but it hadn't really been a drawing. She'd been here only six months, replacing Cat Henderson, who had apparently been quite popular among the deputies. Plus, being so new, Candy couldn't expect to do anything major until she'd been assessed.

Anyway, here she was, assigned to assist a ghost hunter, of all things. To be a liaison. To smooth his way and maybe keep him out of trouble.

Not that she really minded. Ghost hunting seemed like a scam to her, but there was no reason helping couldn't be fun. As October settled in fully, with Halloween looming, the shorter days and the atmosphere might add to the spookiness. Or at least those were her arguments for making the assignment more palatable.

While she didn't like ghost-hunting TV, she *did* like spookiness and hat strange upside-down magic that held dark promise like a good thriller.

The streets around town were already succumbing. Uncut pumpkins decorated front porches. She looked forward to seeing their carved faces. A few trees dangled sturdy skeletons, and she saw more than one bedsheet ghost. And she always grinned.

A much pleasanter environment than the places she'd visited in the Army. Too often she had to shake herself out of a horrifying memory. A good ghost story might be a relief because she knew all about *real* ghosts.

Velma, the ancient dispatcher, sat on the far side of the room, her headset firmly planted under and around her thinning gray hair. There was a rumor that dispatch was to be moved to a room in the back, but in six months Candy had come to like Velma and her colleagues right where they were. They were company, and their chatter was just as illuminating as the police band radio. Maybe more so because the dispatchers talked to individual patrols, giving Candy better detail. Plus, they could talk to cops who had for some reason moved to cell phones from their radios.

She supposed that in time she'd understand that, too.

Velma suddenly spoke. Her smoke-roughened voice emerged from the ever-present cloud of the cigarettes she frequently smoked right beneath the no-smoking sign.

"This might be your guy, Candy."

Candy turned her attention to the front door. Oh, yeah. The autumn clothes fit fairly well with the surrounding area, except they looked almost new. No years of wear.

Good-looking guy, too. A face for TV maybe, except not perfect. Those slight imperfections, a scar on his chin and a nose that wasn't perfectly straight, suggested a past that might be almost normal.

"Hi," he said. "I'm sorry I'm late. Had a little car trouble on the way. I'm looking for Deputy Serrano?"

Candy rose immediately from her desk. "Steve Hawks?"

"So they tell me." With an engaging smile, he offered his hand and shook hers. "I wouldn't blame you if you're irritated. I hate to be late, but damn, those mountains just wouldn't move any closer."

She chuckled, knowing exactly what he meant. "For the longest time they just seem to be pulling away. Have a seat, Mr. Hawks."

He sat in the chair beside her desk. Then he came

straight to the point. "I imagine you didn't volunteer for this assignment."

She didn't know quite how to answer that. Nothing seemed politic.

"I like a link with the local police," he went on. "I want facts, not fiction, and a lot of what people think is true just isn't."

She had no trouble understanding that. Already she began to like him. Facts, not fiction, seemed like a good motto. "I prefer facts myself." She hoped that didn't sound like a challenge, but it probably did. Too bad.

The door swung open, admitting a uniformed deputy named Connie Parish. She flashed a grin as she headed toward the break room. "Seems like you're sitting right where Cat used to sit." Without a pause, she kept striding toward the back.

What did that mean? Candy wondered as she returned her attention to the puzzle named Steve.

"Do you know the Castelle family?" he asked. "I'm here to interview them."

"I know of them. I don't think I've talked to them except in passing." Were they subjects for his show? That was hard to believe considering she'd often seen the adults outside playing with a young daughter and a growing dog. A normal, happy family. Not one shadowed by uneasy things.

Now her interest was piqued. "Do they have a ghost problem?"

"That's what I'm here to find out. I'd love to debunk it for them." He glanced at his watch, then rose. "I need to check in at the motel. How about we have dinner somewhere so you can grill me along with a steak?"

He probably had an expense account, she decided.

So yeah, she'd hit him up for a dinner. "You have two good choices in this town. The truck stop grill or Maude's place. Good food at both."

He arched a brow. "That's it?"

"The Mexican restaurant hasn't opened yet, but we do have a burger place and a pizzeria on the edge of town. The burgers are okay, Maude's are better. Pizza?" She shrugged, hardly a recommendation. "Both are popular hangouts for young people. Oh, yeah, how could I forget Mahoney's Bar? Great sandwiches and fried chicken."

Steve nodded, apparently accepting the limitations. "I'll meet you at Maude's at six, then. I can get directions at the motel."

She pointed straight out the window. "The café is thataway, a half block. The City Diner, the sign says, but everyone calls it Maude's."

"Been here forever, huh?"

"Maybe two forevers."

That elicited a bark of laughter from him as he headed toward the door.

"Seems like an okay guy," Velma remarked, then went back to her duties, acknowledging an officer on the radio who was making a traffic stop outside town.

An okay guy? Maybe. Since he was a television star, Candy withheld judgment and just hoped she didn't meet a soaring ego.

DESPITE HIS TARDINESS, Steve thought he had started on a decent path with Deputy Serrano. He'd sensed only a mild resistance, for which he couldn't blame her. Babysitting a reality TV personality wasn't on most people's top-ten list.

On the other hand, he really liked to get the police involved as much as he could. Even one on-screen interview of a cop providing information could prove extremely revealing, and it certainly lent credence to his investigation. If Serrano didn't want to do it, she might well know someone who would.

He'd like to get her, though. She was a pretty Latina he judged would photograph well.

What the hell did a guy wear to a dinner at a café in this town? Dress up seemed unlikely from his minor scoping as he drove in. He settled on jeans and a white dress shirt. Without a tie, and with sleeves rolled up, it became casual.

Dang, he could remember times when he never had to think of such things. As a plainclothes detective, he'd needed only a couple of suits and a whole bunch of clean shirts.

Big deal. The clock said he had a little time to unpack, not that there was much. During the next few weeks, he didn't need anything that couldn't be cleaned in a coin laundry. When his production team came, they'd bring more with them.

Then he sat in the chair beside the small table and looked around at the room. Someone had tried to modernize it, but large-purchase bedding and lamps from a supply house didn't quite make it. Chosen to be inoffensive, they practically blended in with the motel-room background. The walls, however, were solid wood planks, not paneling.

Not that he minded. He'd slept in worse places because the show did have a budget. One hotel was expensive? Then find something cheaper at the next location. He didn't think the La-Z-Rest motel was going to break any bank.

And why didn't this motel give itself a face-lift with a new name? It was so 1950s. All it lacked was a sputtering neon sign. No sputtering here.

Sighing, eager to be doing something besides sitting on his can, especially after a long day in the car, he pulled out his slim leather portfolio and looked at the numbers he needed to call. The Castelles first. They were the ones who were worried enough to call him.

His major goal in this was to ease a little girl's mind. The seven-year-old had the problem and her parents didn't know how to handle it. They'd tried everything, they'd explained the first time he talked to them.

His secondary goal was to ensure no one was after the family, and that neither parent was frightening the daughter for some end of his or her own. He'd been a cop too long to overlook such possibilities.

He hoped they didn't necessarily want a paranormal explanation. He'd need actual proof before he could do that, and thus far he'd almost never needed those words: *I don't know what it is.*

Paranormal. Damn, this country had begun to fall into a state of belief.

HALF AN HOUR later he decided to stretch his legs by walking to the diner. He'd left a voice mail with the Castelles and said he'd call in the morning. Now he wanted to make the deputy a little less dubious about him. He didn't need her trust, but he *did* need her co-operation.

With night falling, the air had grown chillier. Fine by him. Except for catastrophic weather, the mostly steady climate of Southern California had become boring. Pleasant but boring. Every now and then he got a little jolt when he was reminded that other places rolled through seasons that were different.

Not that he wanted to be shoveling snow for months on end, but he enjoyed the changes when he ran into them.

When he reached the diner, he spied Deputy Serrano sitting at a table right in front of the window. She had twisted to look up at a man who stood beside her and spoke with expansive gestures. She was smiling.

All to the good, Steve thought as he moved between tables to reach her. The place was crowded, which spoke well of the food. His stomach rumbled, reminding him that he'd skipped lunch because he was late.

Delicious aromas filled the room. The clatter of utensils and plates joined with various conversations. The diner felt friendly.

By the time he reached Serrano, the man had moved on. When she saw Steve, she gave him a polite smile. Just that, nothing more. At the same time, she pointed to the chair across from her.

He slid in and leaned back, hoping not to make her feel crowded at this small table. "Hi," he said as she passed him a plastic-covered menu. Surprised fingers told him it was clean, not greasy or sticky as he would have expected.

The woman who brought him coffee, a rather large angry-looking person, slammed down cups and began filling them with coffee. "Back soon," she grumped and stalked away.

Steve couldn't help but raise a brow in Serrano's direction.

Her faint smile widened a bit. "Maude, the owner. Consider her to be part of the local color."

"Does she hate running this place that much?"

The deputy shook her head. "I don't think so. She's been here for nearly fifty years."

Well, that was a puzzle, he thought as he scanned the menu. Not a bad selection for a place so small. Most of it could be cooked on a grill, another time-saver.

"Any recommendations?" he asked Serrano.

"Just about anything. In fact, everything."

He looked at her and she shrugged.

"I've only been here six months," she said. "Long enough to say I've never had a bad meal. Long enough to add that eating here, while delicious, makes your arteries cringe."

That was okay by Steve. He usually ate healthy stuff, but he didn't mind going off the wagon occasionally. Else how could a man get a large rare steak? Or a really good pork chop?

Or even some fries. He had a weakness for them.

After they ordered, he eyed the deputy across the table. She didn't seem all that eager to indulge in casual conversation, which was fine. Her eyes, however, actively scanned the room. Alert.

When they were served, she with a burger, he with a steak sandwich, she sighed.

"I'm sorry, Mr. Hawks. I'm not freezing you, but I just don't know what to talk about. How about business?"

"Call me Steve."

One corner of her mouth tipped up. "I'm Candy. What are we supposed to do here?"

"Well, I'm here for the next few weeks ahead of my

production crew. I need to speak with the Castelle family, find out their whole story and gain some rapport with their daughter."

"Meaning?" She held half the burger in her hand.

Steve took her cue and picked up part of his steak sandwich. "She's only seven, Candy. Talking with a stranger won't be easy for her. But I need *her* to tell me what's troubling her, not what her parents think is bothering her."

She nodded, taking a bite out of her burger and dabbing at some escaped juice.

"So that is one of my first goals. Second, I need to get in the weeds on any local lore that could possibly be related, and probably into some local history. I need to build a picture of what might be going on here."

She nodded, then snagged a fresh napkin to wipe her mouth again. "And what will you do with this picture?"

"It's my hope to find some banal answer to the problem. To be able to reassure that family and the little girl that nothing bad is happening and they can ignore all this."

She blinked. "You don't want a ghost?"

"I'd really rather not. I hate it when I can't come up with a better explanation."

"Wild."

For the first time he saw her face relax, as if she were letting go of an internal tension. *One hurdle cleared*, he thought.

"But how can you make a ghost show without finding a ghost?" she asked, a perfectly reasonable question.

He replied firmly: "My goal has never been to find ghosts. What I want to do is reassure terrified families who think they've reached the limit of plausible explanations. And if I can't debunk the ghost idea, then I want at the very least to be able to reassure them they have nothing to fear."

"But couldn't you just say that?"

He shook his head. "They've already been saying it to themselves. If nothing else, they can see me do a complete investigation to assure them there's nothing there."

"But how can you do a ghost show if that's your purpose?" She repeated her question, and he sensed she needed more.

He wiped his own mouth and leaned forward a bit. "Because I'm doing a show about people who *believe* they have ghosts. I take them seriously."

CANDY DECIDED HE might not be the con artist she expected. He had a different twist on the subject matter, or at least different from what she'd expected. Of course, if he was conning her, she probably wouldn't know at first. Time to keep the radar up. Trust him? Trust didn't come easily to her.

But if what he said was true, then he wasn't simply out to create a spectacle with a family and their problems.

"Why does it have to be done on TV, though?" She hoped that didn't offend him, because if it did the next few weeks were going to be tough.

"It's simple," he answered as he reached for a home fry. "When I was a cop, I noticed a continuing uptick in the number of calls that people blamed on the paranormal. I couldn't do anything except tell them they didn't have a prowler, nobody was in the house, maybe they needed a plumber, and then I'd have to move on. The people were still afraid, and sometimes they'd call several times with the same complaint."

She shook her head a little bit. "That must have been frustrating."

"To some. It troubled me. These people weren't getting any help from us, and we're supposed to be able to help."

"Good point." Partly, at least. There really wasn't something a cop could do sometimes.

He finished the fry and reached for another. "Anyway, after a while, on my off-duty time, I went back to talk to these folks and tried to work with them. What with one thing and another, this production company approached and offered me a series. I didn't want to do it at first, but they made it obvious that I could do a whole lot more helping if I had the money for it and didn't have another full-time job. I told them I would, but only if they weren't expecting paranormal answers."

"And they agreed to that?" The notion surprised her. She wouldn't have expected it.

He tipped his head to one side briefly, an almost shrug. "They thought it would be an original spin. Three seasons later, I have to think they were right."

"It seems so." Her appetite had returned in full force, and she looked down at the burger on her plate. It looked better now than when Maude had slammed it onto the table. Yup. She lifted it, ready to finish it.

Candy felt, too, a whole lot better about what was to come. They continued to eat for a while before she asked, "Have you ever found a ghost?"

"Not anything I'd take to the bank. I wouldn't exactly mind if I found some good evidence, except that it would turn my worldview upside down and give it a good shaking."

She laughed, liking that. "It would for me, too."

Considering this assignment was going to be close to a month long, any positive she could find would help. It might be fun in more ways than just watching this all unfurl. Steve Hawks seemed to have a sense of humor, which made almost anything easier to deal with.

She also had an inkling that the success of his show wasn't entirely dependent on what he found, or the stories he told. No, he had charisma, the kind that would draw viewers along the paths he wove with his storytelling.

A unique kind of storytelling, she suspected. Unlike some of the ghost shows she had watched briefly, where a dash of history and a lot of "Did you hear that?" failed to tell a tale of any kind. Lots of supposition, little substance.

"Are you a fan of paranormal shows?" he asked.

"I stuck my toes in for a while. Curiosity. But I haven't tuned in recently."

"You're not missing much," he admitted, then flashed the most charming grin.

Damn, she could understand why people kept watching. She suspected his fan mail was positively steamy. She certainly needed to avoid that reaction.

Pushing her plate to one side, Candy reached for her coffee. She was one of the lucky ones—or unlucky, depending—that caffeine didn't keep awake. Sometimes at one in the morning she had wished it would.

"WHAT ABOUT YOU?" Steve asked. "You said you've been here only six months?"

She nodded. "Army. Discharged over a year ago."

"Army, huh?" He felt surprised, though he couldn't say why. Maybe because he'd thought she'd been a cop for a long time, like him. "What did you do?"

Then he saw her face harden, her eyes grown distant. For several beats she didn't answer, and when she did her voice sounded tight.

"Too much."

He let it drop, intuiting that there were memories she didn't want to revive, and he didn't want to push her there.

His view of her altered, however. She had a background that only someone who'd been there could ever fully understand. His work as a cop didn't come close. How could it?

He wasn't an insensitive man. His ability to empathize had often caused him difficulty in his own work. Cops didn't like to talk about it, but most had strong feelings when it came to victims and their families. Some cases even became downright personal. First responders could rarely stay detached no matter how hard they tried.

To that extent, he understood how memories could ride your thoughts or become buried until they surfaced suddenly in a nightmare or were resurrected by another situation.

He sought safer ground. "How do you like working here?"

Her faint smile returned as if she had swept something aside. "So far, so good. People are great, the job is mostly routine. I've still got a lot to learn, obviously, but everyone in the office is being really nice about my inexperience."

"Sounds like a good group of people."

"The best. I'm filling some big shoes, though."

He arched a brow and resisted the urge to eat another home fry. *But why?* he asked himself. *Why not have one?* He helped himself. "Whose shoes?"

"My predecessor. She was with the department for over two years, then left to follow her Army husband to his post."

"Not a very liberated thing to do."

Candy laughed. It had been the right note to hit.

Then she answered. "On the surface, maybe not. But she found another police job, and I can understand why she wants to be close. They hadn't been married for long."

"That does make a difference from what I've seen."

Now it was her turn to look quizzically at him. "Never tried it?"

"Me? Not yet. I'm like a ton of bricks. Someone will need to knock me over."

"Maybe with a feather?"

He liked that. "Absolutely with a feather. Make easy work of me."

He drew a chuckle from her and decided they were moving to comfortable ground.

"What do you need me for?" she asked.

"Any difficulties that might come up when we start filming. Not from people so much as the authorities around here. I need to know if we're getting out of line. Toes must not be stepped on."

Candy nodded. "Anything else?"

"Smoothing introductions so people don't see me as a suspicious stranger. Any advice you can give along the way about where I should look or who I should talk to."

"Reasonable."

Maude made another banging round and refreshed their coffee.

"Amazing," Steve murmured, looking down.

"Good food," Candy answered. "From what I understand she's always been like this, and her daughter Mavis is doing a good job as copycat. Anyway, I think folks have been used to it for a long time."

He could see that, but being an outsider he wondered if he'd ever get used to it. It was a slightly disturbing punctuation to a meal.

He'd been a people watcher for much of his adult life, though. A bit of a character collector. He added Maude to his mental file.

Candy cradled her coffee mug as if warming her hands. "What do you need a deputy for? Wouldn't someone else be in a better position?"

"Evidently not. We contacted county and city officials and they referred us to you."

Another smile flitted across her face. "Cowards."

He grinned again. "Most politicians are."

A while later, after Steve had overindulged with a piece of the best peach pie he'd ever tasted, they parted ways outside, agreeing to meet at the sheriff's office at nine the next morning.

He started walking back to the motel, then decided a little more local atmosphere would be good. It was almost Halloween, and the pumpkins and pretend ghosts drew him. Shoving his hands into the pockets of his jacket, he began a lazy stroll more to see the way the town looked than to admire uncarved pumpkins.

There were old enough neighborhoods where he came from, but they weren't entire towns like this one. He imagined roots around here, deep as the largest tree, tying everyone together.

Very cool. He liked it.

BEN WITTES SAW the stranger as he was walking past the Conard County Sheriff's Office. His interest perked immediately.

He wondered if this guy was the ghost show host who was rumored to be coming to town. Maybe so.

As a psychic, Ben thought he might be able to help the guy out. After all, he was able to communicate with spirits. He did it all the time.

Go for it, whispered one of the spirits. Maybe his guide.

Yeah, he'd go for it. He could provide information that they'd never find for the show.

Now all he had to do was wait for the opportunity.

Smiling, Ben continued his stroll, feeling pretty good. This was his opportunity to make a splash with his skills.

Chapter Two

In the morning, Candy looked out her window at a perfect autumn day. While she loved sunshine as much as anyone, the low scudding clouds, dark with their hint of a threat, were appealing given the season.

She laughed quietly at herself as she donned her uniform for another day on the job. She really did like it here, and the longer she stayed, the more she liked it.

Just last evening, after her dinner with Steve Hawks, she joined some women at the library for their book group. They met once a week for discussion, and those meetings turned into a lot more than book reports. Laughter filled their room, someone always brought baked goods, and they wound up talking about families and sometimes jobs.

She had started to make friends. A good feeling, especially when she was still easing her way into this new job and new town. Everyone at the office was friendly, but it wasn't the same, not when she felt she was under a microscope. Superficially that didn't seem true, but she couldn't help thinking it. It wasn't as if she had any prior experience in the police.

Candy was still surprised that she'd been hired. She'd been bouncing around since her discharge, aware that infantry training and combat experience weren't exactly marketable skills. Some private security firms had wanted her, but deep inside she'd felt, maybe mistakenly, that she would become a mercenary. A soldier for hire.

Then, taking a flier, she had applied for this job when she read about it in the classifieds online. Six weeks later, after an interview, she'd been hired.

Yep, that amazed her. When she expressed her astonishment to the sheriff, Gage Dalton, he'd laughed. "It's kind of a tradition around here. We already know you're brave, able to work in teams and trainable. We can do the training."

Maybe she'd found her place.

She popped out to walk to work. She liked the weather, she liked the nip in the air. Uncarved pumpkins didn't exactly look cheery in this light, nor did the lack of Halloween lights. For now, the street was not lined with bright pops of orange. A dismal but gorgeous day.

Candy closed her eyes momentarily and smelled the air, listening to the sounds as a breeze brushed more dying leaves around. Perfect.

Yeah, perfect for a ghost hunt. She grinned into the chilly breeze, wondering what the days ahead held. For the first time in years, anticipation didn't bring dread. Her internal pressure valve had begun to release.

She was still smiling when she reached the office. Guy Redwing, a friendly dude, sat behind the duty desk and greeted her pleasantly. "How's it going, Candy?"

"Just fine," she answered, then waved to Velma as she passed her. The coffee urn usually held battery acid, but there was a pot of hot water and plenty of tea bags. A foam cup filled with English breakfast tea was only a few minutes away.

The office appeared empty this morning, and she returned to Guy with her cup, asking, "Something going on?"

He shook his head. "No coffee klatch this morning. There was apparently a lot of vandalism last night."

"Really? There hasn't been much since I got here."

He snorted. "You haven't been here long enough. Halloween brings out something crazy in the kids. Anyway, the vandalism isn't usually earthshaking. Mostly egged cars, some spray painting of scary faces at the schools. So far I haven't heard that they've sprayed anybody's house."

"Well, that's good."

"If we catch some of them, they'll get a workout with deck brushes."

She thought that sounded like a great idea, better than fines or suspended sentences.

"Oh, yeah," Guy added. "Did I mention at least two houses have been toilet-papered?"

"At least?" Candy sat in the chair beside his desk, holding her tea in her hand.

"Yeah. At least. And there may be more before we move into Thanksgiving season. Anyway, I'm sure we haven't gotten all the reports yet."

"That toilet papering has to be miserable to clean up."

Guy flashed a wide grin and mimicked an evil laugh. "Not if we find the perps. The nice thing about kids this age? They don't know when to shut their mouths. I'm sure we'll start to find them bragging online before long."

Candy had to chuckle even though apprehension began to niggle at her. Steve Hawks would appear at any minute and, even after their dinner last night, she still wouldn't trust him any farther than she could throw him. He'd made a reasoned case for what he was doing, but he was still here and still about to put a family's fears on television. And to make money from it.

There was no escaping that.

Oh, well, she'd get through this as cheerfully as she could. Being a good soldier was one way to look at it. She'd do her duty, whether she liked it or not.

Then the man himself walked through the door with a rush of cold air. Today Steve wore his leather bomber jacket zipped up, and she couldn't help wondering how cold it would have to get before he decided he needed a jacket or coat that would cover his butt.

"Hi," he said with a smile. "Ready to go?"

"Where to?" Candy asked, rising from her chair and tossing her empty cup in a nearby trash can.

"To visit the Castelles. Ten o'clock appointment. But hey, is there anywhere convenient I can get a decent take-out coffee?"

That surprised her. "Haven't you eaten yet? Everyone serves coffee."

"Not enough for me. Maude's?"

"Absolutely."

"Come with?" he asked, raising a brow. "Or meet you back here."

She decided to go with him. Another chance to walk ahead of what she feared would become a problematic day. The wind hit her smack in the face when she stepped outside.

"Whew," she exclaimed. "When did that happen?"

"The wind or the cold?"

She glanced at him askance. "What do you think?"

"Ha. You want some coffee, too?"

After they got two tall cups full of steaming coffee, Candy asked, "Do you want me to follow in my patrol car, or do you want to ride along? Whichever you think would least worry the family."

He paused to look down at her. "Why would they worry? They know who I am."

She just shook her head, wondering if this was a taste of his ego. "The face recognized around the world?"

That darkened his expression just a bit. "They knew who I was when they contacted me. I've spent hours on the phone with them. I am not exactly a stranger."

She couldn't really argue with that. At this point, the Castelles probably felt they knew him better than any local cop. Especially her. Waving from a patrol car as she drove by and exchanging a few words with them at the end of their driveway hardly constituted any kind of relationship.

"I'll follow," she answered briskly, warning herself not to make quick assumptions about any of this. That wasn't part of the job, nor was needlessly annoying him.

Outside the sheriff's office, she climbed into her official SUV and backed out. She didn't exactly need to follow him because she knew where the Castelles lived. He would, too, assuming his GPS navigator worked. Which was often hit-or-miss in some places around here.

The Castelles didn't live very far out of town. They had moved into an older house on some acreage. It had a barn, which could still be useful if they wanted to renovate it, and the house was only one story. Except this one had a steeply sloped, high roof with some windows that suggested the attic could be used as living space.

She wished she could find out. She'd always felt some appeal in finished attics, although she'd have been hard-pressed to explain it. She certainly had never lived in a house with one.

Sometimes her own brain made her wonder.

Steve arrived without a problem and pulled into the long asphalt driveway. Not sure what to do at this point, Candy parked on the shoulder near the mailbox. If anyone wanted or needed her, she'd be in plain view. Sipping her coffee, grateful for its warmth, she kept an eye on the house.

She saw Steve walk up to the front door, then disappear inside. This was *not* going to be an exciting morning for her.

Steve greeted Anabelle Castelle with a warm smile. He hardly needed her to introduce herself since he'd already seen her on the video she'd provided. Dark hair, blue eyes, and a classic face with great bone structure that was looking a little frayed around the edges. She wore a blue flannel shirt over black slacks.

"Where are all the people?" Anabelle asked. "I was expecting an invasion."

"Sorry. Didn't I tell you? I come alone first. It makes it easier for us to talk. I need to meet the three of you, then start looking into some background."

She nodded, leading him toward a living room. "Have a seat. I'll get Todd." She paused as she turned, giving him a tired smile. "I always like the history part of your show best."

"Thanks." he replied. "You look tired. Do you want me to come back another time?"

She shook her head. "We had a rough night last night. There are quite a few of them these days."

Todd Castelle looked haggard, too, as he joined them. An average-size guy with the light brown hair that often indicated someone who had been blond once upon a time. His dark-haired wife had the blue eyes, though. He had the gray.

"Why is a cop parked out front?" Todd asked. "Is something wrong?"

Steve hastened to reassure them. "She's my minder. They call her a liaison." He gave a light laugh. "I don't know if she's supposed to help me as much as she's supposed to reassure the people I talk to."

"Well, she shouldn't have to sit out there," Annabelle said.

Todd agreed. "I'll go out and get her."

"And I'll make some coffee," his wife replied. "It's getting chilly in here. You sure that heat is working?"

"Honey, it's set to sixty-eight."

"Yeah, but I still get cold." She rose while Todd headed to the door and gave Steve a wry look. "We argue about this year-round. I'm either too hot or too cold, and he's always just right. Must be hormonal differences."

Steve wouldn't have stepped into that potential minefield for anything, not once hormones were mentioned. But he chuckled, the safe response.

He also wished they weren't bringing Candy into this. He needed the time getting to know his clients without their holding anything back because someone else was listening.

Oh, hell, he'd make up for this somehow. There'd be another interview, one without Candy, he hoped. Not that he didn't like her well enough, considering they'd just met, but she was still an official, a cop, and few people wanted to be wholly frank while a cop listened.

He ought to know. His years on the force weren't *that* far behind him.

Candy entered with Todd, gently refusing coffee, holding up her take-out cup as if in explanation. Soon Anabelle had them all seated in the living room, the aromas of fresh-brewed coffee filling the air.

Steve waited a minute, then said, "Would you mind walking me through everything again? I want to be sure I haven't missed something."

Annabelle looked surprised. "I thought we would do that on the show."

"You will, but we'll have to edit it for length. You won't be able to give me all the details then, but I need to be sure *I* don't miss something. With or without the show, I'll investigate fully. You can always back out anytime you want."

Todd and Annabelle exchanged looks. Todd nodded and spoke. "That's what we agreed to. And if we change our minds, you'll still investigate?"

"Thoroughly. That's how I got into this business in the first place."

Todd looked satisfied. "The intro to the show says you're a former homicide detective."

"That's right. Twelve years as a detective, and before that I was a patrol officer. I can tell you which was more interesting."

That drew a small laugh from Annabelle. "The intro also says that you got into this because of your policing."

"Not exactly. I was increasingly disturbed by the number of people who called in complaints of paranormal activity. And I was limited in what I could do. Check the premises, check the yard. It was no help at all. That's when I started going back when I was off duty to see if I could do more."

Annabelle tilted her head. "You really care that much?"

"That's how I wound up here. And that's why I'm willing to go ahead with this investigation even if you decide not to do the show."

For the first time, Candy spoke. "That's remarkable."

Steve noted there wasn't a touch of sarcasm in her comment. Maybe he was persuading her that he wasn't a con artist.

He wasn't sure about the Castelles, however. Yes, they'd called him. Yes, they'd said they would do this. But now they were looking down the barrel of having to appear on a nationally televised show. A lot of people didn't want to take their crazy stories public.

Then Todd surprised him. "I'm a graphic artist for comic books. Annabelle writes them. Any of our friends won't be surprised if we get wacky over this."

"It's true," Annabelle agreed. "We're already off-center, living in a world of superheroes and magic powers. Heck, this could be one of my scripts."

This time it was Steve who wondered about *them*. What if *they* weren't on the up-and-up? What if they saw some free publicity?

Oh, hell, a new wrinkle. But he didn't let those thoughts show on his face. One thing about being a homicide detective, you learned to control your face and emotions unless they'd be helpful.

"Anyway," Todd said, "I don't see any reason, at least not yet, why we'd back out of the show."

Steve returned to his original question. "Can you tell me all about it? Would you prefer to have Officer Serrano wait outside?"

"Why?" Todd asked bluntly. "We're proposing to take this to TV. Might as well get used to telling the world."

Annabelle sighed. "Where do you want me to start? Why we moved here?"

Steve nodded.

"Big space, cheaper cost of living. We wanted Viv and her dog to have a place to run that didn't involve a trip to a park. Cheaper because it's not the big city. In our job, we don't make a whole lot, so coming here let us have more room and still live within our budget. Maybe less crime. I suppose time will answer that question."

Steve spoke. "And now Viv's afraid."

Todd replied. "That's killing us. We brought her here to give her a freer life but she's scared all the time."

Then the story began to tumble out of them. He'd heard most of it on the phone, but he was looking for details that might have been overlooked.

A couple of months after they moved in, Viv started talking about an invisible man in her bedroom. She said she didn't like him and wanted him to go away. Naturally they tried sleeping in her room with her as opposed to taking her into their bed. They hadn't wanted to encourage fanciful tales that might simply arise from the big move they'd made.

It *had* been a huge change in her life, Annabelle said, and since moving was a great stressor even on adults, she had at first assumed that was what was going on.

But when they stayed in the room, they heard nothing and saw nothing. Things quieted down, and Viv seemed to go back to normal.

But then it started again. "The man keeps talking to me!"

Followed by Todd and Annabelle taking turns sleeping in her room with her. Neither of them heard anything and tried to ease their way back to a more usual arrangement.

Once again everything quieted, until the night Viv refused to calm even when they stayed with her. She began screaming and crying for them to make the man go away. Whereas she'd been afraid only at night before, her terror seemed to grow until she refused to even play in her room.

Todd and Annabelle were totally perplexed. Viv was okay playing in the yard with her puppy, or playing in another room they had turned into a playroom, but she refused to go into her own bedroom. A handful of times she went back in there to get something she wanted, and entirely too often would come out and claim the man had talked to her again.

But Viv had no idea what he might be saying. None. She just didn't like his voice and especially didn't like him being invisible.

Eventually the Castelles had begun to wonder if their daughter had a serious problem. They took her to a highly recommended child psychologist.

That impressed Steve. In his experience, most parents didn't want to believe their children might have a psychological problem. The shame frightened them, as if they would turn out to be failures as parents. It often prevented action. But not for the Castelles.

After six weeks of making the lengthy trip to see the psychologist, they got an answer that wasn't entirely reassuring.

Annabelle continued with the story. "The psychologist said there was absolutely nothing wrong with Viv. That it was a phase, maybe precipitated by our move, but she'd grow out of it."

Steve felt a burst of sympathy. "Did that make you feel better?" He suspected it hadn't.

"No," Todd said bluntly. "He told us our kid isn't mentally ill, which is great, but that she was just acting out. And while I'm no psychologist, I heard a subtext."

"Which was?"

"Our daughter is having emotional problems, but temporary. That's not a lot of string to hang on to."

Steve set his coffee aside on an end table and leaned forward until his elbows rested on his knees. He clasped his hands, thinking and absorbing.

"Okay," he said presently. "That wasn't the end of it, though."

"Of course not," Todd said. "I'd already checked the basement for banging pipes, humming things, anything that might reach her room from below. Nothing. But I went and checked it all again. Useless. Hell, I even went up into the attic where there's no plumbing or wiring except for several bulbs at the top of the stairs."

Annabelle spoke again. "In one way I think that psychologist was all wet. Viv's not acting out. If she were doing that, she'd be acting out in every other room in this house. She'd even act out at school some-times. She's not."

Todd nodded agreement. "That doesn't seem like a useful explanation."

"It's not," Annabelle said firmly. "What's more, the problem didn't go away."

Steve waited. "How did you know that?"

"Because Viv walked by her bedroom one evening and said she heard the man singing."

"Singing!" That startled Steve a bit. It was a new claim to him. Crying, yes. Shouting, yes. Talking, knocking, moving things, but this was the first he'd heard of singing.

"Yeah," said Todd almost wryly. "Weird. Weirder than the rest." He sighed, passing a hand over his face. "Then Annabelle…" He broke off. "I'll let her tell it."

"I heard it, too," she said quietly. "Just once. I'd gone into Viv's room to get some of her winter clothes, and I heard it. It *did* sound like a man talking, but from far away. He didn't sound as if he were in the room." She shook her head. "I felt like ice water ran down my spine. I raced to get Todd, but by the time we both came back, it had stopped. Then I noticed something else I hadn't really paid attention to before."

"That was?"

"Viv's dog was in there, and he was growling at the wall with his hackles up. I'd never seen him do that be-fore. Or if he had, there in her room, I hadn't noticed. Then I noticed him doing it more often."

Steve had some familiarity as a cop with a dog's heightened senses. They could detect things that hu-mans couldn't. But more than that, they usually knew when something was a threat. More trouble.

"Anyway," Todd continued, "we started paying attention to Buddy. Most of the time he didn't seem disturbed. He was happy, prancing around the house, playing with Viv. But every now and then he'd react to something in her bedroom. Not constantly, just sometimes."

Steve waited expectantly. He thought he knew the rest, but he wanted to hear it again. Much could be revealed by faces that wouldn't necessarily come across in a phone call. He was getting the close-up look he needed.

"Viv," said Annabelle. "It's getting worse, Steve. She doesn't want to even walk by her bedroom. She begged us to get rid of the man. Do you know what it's like to have your daughter desperately begging you for something you can't give her?"

While Steve had no children, he didn't have any trouble imagining how awful the Castelles must be feeling. "Are you still sleeping with her?"

"She's in our bed every night now, and some nights she doesn't sleep at all because she was terrified the man would come out of her room and find her."

It was definitely getting worse, Steve thought. For Viv, and for them.

Todd spoke. "Anyway, I decided I had to do something. Anything."

Annabelle jumped in. "Maybe we're being crazy. I don't know."

Steve replied, hoping he could reassure this couple. Their pain wrenched at his heart. "I'd be going crazy, too."

Annabelle gave him a faint smile. "We watched some ghost shows from time to time. We're not avid, but we think they're fun. Or we did until this. Anyway, EMF…"

Electromagnetic frequencies. They could affect the brain and cause weird experiences. He was familiar with them.

Todd joined in. "I got us an EMF meter just before we called you. We figured that since the voice was confined to Viv's room, there might be something like that going on. She might be extremely sensitive. The dog, too. It might also explain the voice Annabelle heard that once. But either way I didn't want Viv in there if some electrical frequency was messing with her brain. Or maybe causing some disease. I thought I'd checked all the wiring, but I didn't get inside the walls. We had to know."

"Good decision," Steve said. "*Excellent* decision and I'm not just saying that because I hunt this stuff. This is something important you need to clear up for Viv's sake."

"That's what we think," Annabelle said. "I sure wasn't about to consider an exorcism or something. Not then, not now, unless you find a reason. Calling it paranormal is the last thing we want to do."

Steve straightened. "You know I try to debunk. That's my main goal. What I want is for people not to be afraid."

"That's why we called you," Todd said. "If you can debunk this, we're going to find a better psychologist. Someone needs to help Viv, and she's become convinced there's ghost in her room."

Steve frowned. Kids. They were incredibly honest about many things, and he didn't think it was likely

Viv was exaggerating her fear or making up the story. "Did you find any EMF?"

Todd answered. "Some but not above a normal level. And no more in Viv's bedroom than in the rest of the house."

Steve decided he had gleaned about all he could from this first interview. Maybe the most important thing had been observing the Castelles. They were genuinely concerned about their daughter. They weren't exaggerating their claims, nothing about dark figures and black mists. They weren't even claiming to be tormented themselves. A very focused investigation on their parts.

"You've done well," he told them. "I'm impressed."

Both parents looked mildly relieved.

"Okay," he said. "I may want to ask you more a little later, but I need to meet Viv. And the dog." He smiled. "If you don't mind, that is, but it'll help me to hear from her what she's experiencing and what she thinks is going on. To do that, I'm going to have to gain her trust so that she feels free to talk to me. Do you mind?"

"Of course not!" Annabelle exclaimed. "For heaven's sake, the entire reason we called you was for help. And one of the things we discussed was whether you could talk to Viv without encouraging her fears. We believe you can."

That was a big vote of confidence, Steve thought. A huge one. "When can I meet her?"

"How much time do you need?"

"As much as she'll give me at our first meeting. It has to be fluid. She sets the boundaries. And where is the dog?"

Todd smiled faintly. "Out in the back in his run."

"Can I meet him? Is he friendly?"

At that, Todd laughed. "He's so friendly he'd love a burglar to death inside our front door. Buddy would knock him over because he so big and kiss him until the burglar begged for mercy. We're still trying to teach the dog not to jump on people when he wants their attention."

Steve grinned. "What's the breed?"

"Half American Staffordshire, and about half bloodhound."

"Big, then. Interesting mix." But Steve glanced at his watch and realized the Castelles had been talking with him for the last three hours. "Listen, you two probably need some sleep, so I'll leave you to it. Tomorrow you can tell me what was so awful about the last few nights, introduce me to Buddy and tell me when's a good time meet Viv. Okay?"

Ten minutes later, he and Candy were outside.

Chapter Three

Outside, just as they reached Steve's car, Candy asked him if he needed her for anything else. She figured if he was off for the rest of the day, she could go back to the office and find something useful to do.

Man, she had felt like a fifth wheel in there. Nothing to contribute, just an observer. She was really surprised the Castelles had invited her inside. Surely they hadn't wanted an audience.

Steve spoke. "You don't have to stay with me every minute."

She shrugged. He might be right, but he also might be wrong. She hadn't received any other assignment. Unless he said he was going to work at the motel, she needed to stay. "You're my detail."

He grimaced. "I didn't want that. If I'd wanted a full-time assistant, I'd have brought one along. I'm sure you have a whole bunch of things to do that are more important than shepherding me around."

Candy felt a flicker of amusement. "I understand why you might not want that. But I'm equally certain the city fathers didn't toss this to the sheriff because they wanted you rolling through here like a loose cannon. I guess I'm the city protection squad. No bad publicity here."

That drew a grin from him. "You might be right. Most of the places I've been to have been too big to worry about it. Not only is Conard City way smaller, but it's also pretty isolated."

"Yup. They'd like to draw more visitors, not drive them away. So please, Steve, make us look good."

The wind kicked up again and she felt her cheeks sting. The frigid warning breath of winter.

"I don't know about you, Candy, but I'm a Southern California guy, and I need to get indoors. I'm going for lunch. If you want to join me, feel free. Me, I'm going to see how many people I can talk to while I eat."

"If you want to talk to locals…"

"Got it. Maude's. See, I learn."

Her entire face relaxed into a smile that seemed to reach all the way through her. She guessed her tension over this guy was easing. She was a long way from trusting him, but she was beginning to believe he wasn't going to be a major headache.

"I'll see you at Maude's," she said, and walked back to her patrol vehicle.

While Candy hated to admit it, even in the privacy of her own mind, he'd impressed her while he was talking with the Castelles. Very sympathetic, supportive. She hadn't heard him trying to persuade them of anything. Not even being on his show.

But there was still a lot of crap. She mulled it over as she drove into town. He was still a ghost hunter. He said he didn't believe in the paranormal, but he was still making his living from it.

As she had seen today, the people who called him

were desperate. Willing to consider, no matter how outlandish, anything that could help them.

That made them vulnerable. Exceedingly vulnerable.

She sighed as she finally pulled into a parking place at the station. For a few minutes, she sat drumming her fingers on the steering wheel as she thought.

She didn't like the whole premise of what Steve was doing, of what the other programs were doing, in fact of the whole field of paranormal investigation. That was a personal prejudice and she knew it.

People were entitled to their own beliefs, of course, but while she'd let them have at it, she didn't have to approve or fail to observe her own beliefs.

At this point, however, this wasn't about beliefs. She'd watched the Castelles talk to Steve. He hadn't fed their concerns. He wanted *their* story. In their own words.

But that didn't mean the Castelles weren't desperate, and desperate people were easy marks. They wanted their daughter to be okay, and at this point if it took someone running around with a recorder and camera, claiming to have heard something or felt some evil spirit, they might well buy it.

Which, as far as Candy could see, wouldn't really help anything.

Giving up trying to escape her own mental gyrations, she left her car and walked toward Maude's. She didn't like this whole idea, didn't like her inchoate position, but that didn't matter. As ill-defined as her assignment was, she still couldn't walk away from it.

And she sure as hell wouldn't walk away until she

was sure that nobody was taking advantage of the Castelles' fears.

Maybe that was her real assignment. Maybe no one thought *Ghostly Ties* would be able to ding the town or county in any measurable way. Maybe they just didn't want a bad outcome for the family.

That wouldn't surprise her. Even in the short time she'd been here, she'd discovered this gossipy little town was very protective of its residents. Even the new ones.

WHEN SHE WALKED through the door of Maude's, the lunch crowd had mostly evaporated, transforming into quieter little groups of people who'd stopped for coffee and maybe a light snack. The usual clatter from the kitchen had quieted as the load lifted. Later this afternoon, activity would spike again.

Steve was seated at the same table they'd occupied last evening, facing the door, a tall coffee in front of him.

She came to join him, but then stopped. A prickle of anxiety hit her, snagging her attention. Then, taking a deep breath, she approached him.

"Hi," he said. "Take a seat."

She hesitated, nearly hating herself for what she was about to say. "Would you mind switching seats? I can't... I don't like to sit with my back to a door."

His brows lifted, then his face gentled. He rose at once. "No problem."

She despised herself for this weakness, but some things had lingered long after she'd come home from the war. This was hardly the worst of it. Unfortunately, it had a way of snapping at her heels when she least expected it.

She slid into the chair that he had just vacated and unzipped her jacket, letting it hang open.

Mavis, Maude's daughter, arrived, pad in hand, with her grumpy expression. "You want coffee? A big one like his?"

She glanced at Steve's take-out cup. More than a mug could hold, but that cup would keep the coffee warm for longer.

"Thanks, Mavis."

Without another word, Mavis trudged away. Unlike her mother, who had the dowdiest dresses in the world, Mavis preferred pants. Jeans, slacks, it didn't matter. Evidently no skirts for her.

"I don't know about you," Steve said, "but I need some lunch." He pushed one of the plastic menus her way. "In fact, I need more than a little lunch. Maybe a big one."

Neither of them said much until their food was delivered. Candy had wanted a salad, but when she considered going home later and cooking herself dinner, she opted for a grilled chicken sandwich. Steve ordered two BLTs.

Instead of separate servings, home fries arrived on a single large plate.

"Thank God," Steve said. "I have such a thing for fried potatoes, and now that they're here, I can't waste them."

Candy laughed, releasing the anxiety that had been dogging her since the moment she'd walked through the door.

"Save me from myself," he said, gesturing toward the potatoes. "Eat some."

He really did have a lot of charm. She also liked

people who could make fun of themselves. But…he was still essentially an unknown.

"What did you think of the Castelles?" he asked, dabbing at his chin with a napkin.

"They seem like very nice people." She wouldn't say more than that. She wasn't about to sit in judgment.

"I thought so," he agreed after he swallowed. "I'm trying to eat my sandwiches and not the fries." Then he picked up a potato and popped it in his mouth. "Not the day for a New Year's resolution."

That drew another laugh from her. "You should do a stand-up routine."

"Not unless I can do it with a plate of fries in hand." He paused. "Seriously, what was your impression? I'm not asking you to judge their character."

She hesitated briefly, then offered what she thought was a safe answer. "They seem very upset."

He nodded. "That was my feeling, too. They weren't feigning their worry."

Her interest spiked. "Have you run into that?"

"Of course. For every ten thousand people who watch these shows, there are another thousand who want to be on them. To star in them. Mostly they're people desperate for attention, but sometimes they're just scammers. I don't know what your time in the Army was like, but I was a cop for a long time. Hell, you get people so desperate for attention that they'll confess to terrible crimes they haven't committed."

"I haven't run into that yet, meaning only that I haven't been a cop for long."

He ate for a little while, then spoke again, thoughtfully. "It's really sad to meet someone like that. I can't imagine feeling that invisible, that unwanted, that uncared-for."

"Is that always what it is?"

He shook his head. "There's a percentage of people who just need to be the center of attention. It doesn't matter how much attention they get otherwise, they're hungry for more. Anyway, that's not the Castelles."

She nibbled some more, then reached for one of the fries. "I can't resist either. And I can always bag my sandwich for home."

He smiled at her. "Dig in. Please."

"But how can you be *sure* that Castelles aren't attention-seeking?"

"My gut. As a detective I had to rely on it, and most of the time I was right. But…I could always be wrong." He also had other concerns, like the *real* family dynamics rather than their public face. Or the possibility that they'd been fleeing, rather than moving. Tonight he'd call a woman who sometimes did research for him, a former cop herself.

"Well," she said, "I thought their concern was genuine. If it wasn't, they deserve an award. They really seem upset about their daughter."

"That caught my attention," he remarked, seeking another potato wedge with his fingers. "I most often hear stories about the entire family being affected. If not the whole family, then most of them. Sometimes it makes me wonder if the ones claiming the experiences are kind of having a bit of group hysteria. As if they've ginned each other up, feeding more and more into the mass experience until it becomes huge. On the other hand, it raises more questions, for me at least, when there's one or two who claim to have experienced nothing."

He shrugged one shoulder. "That's not a metric, of course. The theory is that some people are sensitive and others are not. What I'm getting at is that the Castelles are very focused on what Viv is experiencing, and only Annabelle claims to have had her own experience, just that once. That's unusual."

"I can see that." Which she could even though she hadn't watched any of these programs in quite a while.

"Anyway, I'm inclined to believe kids, even though they can be wonderful liars."

She tilted her head. "Why's that?"

"Because they're almost never *good* liars."

She grinned. "It's true, isn't it? I haven't had a whole lot of time with youngsters recently, but I can still remember how rarely my brother and I could get away with anything."

"That's it. It usually doesn't take long to suss out the truth."

She remembered what Guy Redwing had said just that morning about how the vandals would start talking or bragging online. Even older kids could set a trap for themselves.

Candy couldn't eat another bite, so when Mavis came around to see if they wanted more coffee, she asked for a take-out box.

"What's your plan?" she asked after Steve, too, asked for a box for his remaining sandwich. He just kept plugging at the fries, though, causing her inward amusement.

"Well, I'm going to call the Castelles later to set up a time to talk to their daughter and meet the dog.

And I need to start my local research. Who can I talk to who might give me some interesting data, particularly about that house?"

"I haven't been here very long, but I'd suggest the head librarian, Emmaline Dalton. Everyone refers to her as Miss Emma, though, and I don't know why. I guess I could ask someone. Anyway, her family has been here forever, and she'd probably be a good person to talk to first."

"Okay, then, I'll head on over. Do you need to watch me?"

She laughed. "I'm not sure exactly what I'm supposed to be doing, but yeah, I guess I should."

He winked. "I could imagine far worse people attached to my hip. And I do want your help with local legends and stuff."

"Miss Emma will know far more than me."

"Candy, that's exactly what *I* want from you. Guidance to local fonts of information. Maybe a little research into various crimes. But first I need direction."

FAR FROM BEING annoyed with Candy's determination to follow him, Steve didn't mind it at all. Whether the town had realized it when they made her his liaison, she leant an aura of authority. With her present, people were more likely to trust him.

The only conversation he had worried she might stymie with her presence was his conversation with the Castelles. For everyone else, she was like a seal of approval. Plus, she really might be able to help him with records searches.

If she was willing, of course.

But he also felt some sympathy for her. She may not

have been a cop for long but, especially with her military background, she probably wanted clearer orders and a better view of her mission here. Instead she was basically flying blind.

He'd caught that thing at the diner, however. Her distaste for sitting with her back to the door. That must result from her Army experience, waving like a quiet reminder that this woman had been through a helluva lot. He wondered if she had a bit of PTSD as a result... or more than a bit. Depending on her military postings, she might have a whole lot.

He didn't need to get personal with her in order to do his job, though. The cop in him picked up enough clues to sense the ground ahead, and whether it would be good or bad. The joys of being an experienced detective: his critical mind never shut down. The hail-fellow-well-met surface he wore concealed his lifetime of suspicion.

The library proved to be one of those built by funds from Andrew Carnegie back around the turn of the last century. It wasn't huge, but it stood sturdily against the tests of time with its red brick structure and the concrete lintel engraved with Carnegie's name and the year.

He'd heard that Carnegie had become a philanthropist after he learned what his business partner had done to labor protesters. One could argue that Carnegie, even though he'd been in England at the time, hadn't been unaware. Whatever was true, well over two thousand libraries had been built, and had fed the minds of generations. Not a bad legacy.

He climbed out of his rental, feeling the cold wind grab at him again. Overhead, dark clouds still dragged through the sky like portents. He smiled at himself. He wasn't one to be given to fanciful thoughts. Or maybe he could be at times.

He waited until Candy had parked, then joined him on the front steps.

"I need to get out my warmer jacket," he remarked. "Can you introduce me to Miss Emma?"

Her expression turned wry. "Are you sure you want to put your reputation in my hands?"

"Cute. Let's go."

The library was warmer inside, not surprising, but it wasn't exactly *warm*. Maybe to help preserve the books, maybe to save on energy or maybe because the locals were used to cooler temperatures and nobody wanted to bake.

Candy led the way to the round center desk, the hallmark of an era. From one of the side rooms he heard voices, young voices who seemed to be discussing games. Off in one corner, a woman was reading a storybook to a bunch of very young kids, too young for kindergarten, he surmised.

The middle-aged woman behind the desk was a study in graceful aging. She had the kind of bone structure in her face that would keep her beautiful for decades to come. Her reddish-and-gray hair was caught up in a bun. With those green eyes, he'd have bet she had once been an eye-catching redhead.

"Hi, Candy," she said, looking over the top of the wooden counter. In front of her sat an older computer that probably meant the library had switched to digital cataloging but, nearby, a wooden card catalog still remained. He was old enough to remember searching through one of them to do research when he was in elementary school. Nostalgia breathed through him. Of course, once upon a time he'd believed he'd never give up print books. He liked the smell of them, the weight of a volume in his hands.

He'd lost the battle. His laptop had two e-readers on it.

"Miss Emma," Candy said, "I'd like you to meet Steve Hawks. He's in town to do a ghost-hunting show."

"Yes, I heard." Miss Emma rose, still smiling, and extended a hand across the counter. "We have your earlier programs available on DVDs here."

"I'm flattered." Not really. If his ego could be so easily flattered, self-disgust should overwhelm him. "I understand you have the best brain to pick around here when it comes to local history."

Emma laughed. "I've been here for much of it. My dad was once a judge here, and my family helped found this town. You could say I'm steeped in the history. Always my avocation. Let's go into my office."

Another woman appeared in answer to Emma's call. She came out of the room that was full of young voices.

"Can you take over for me out here, Nora?" Emma asked her.

"Absolutely. My sons will probably enjoy my absence more than my presence."

Emma had a spacious office. Apparently, space strictures didn't apply here. Shelves were filled with books, a few stacks of them decorated a corner, and her desk had very nearly disappeared beneath another computer and a scattering of papers.

"Pardon my desk," she said. "We're still trying to get all the books into the digital catalog."

"Probably one heck of a job," Steve offered.

Emma nodded. "And way past due. Have a seat, both of you."

CANDY TOOK A chair that was farther from the desk than the one Steve chose. She was prepared to listen with half an ear to a subject that didn't especially appeal to her. A little local history? Great. A detailed one? Not necessary for her.

This was a go-nowhere task. She had to suppress a sigh. She wasn't at all sure what Steve needed from her, and not sure what her bosses expected of her, and she wondered if this was going to be much fun at all. She sure as heck didn't feel like she was accomplishing much.

Maybe she ought to just go back to the office, find some work to do and wait for Steve to call her if he needed something. Whatever the town wanted from her, she doubted this was it. Making his path easier? Hey, didn't they have a PR person they could have asked to take on this job?

Impatience was beginning to irritate her. Sure, it had been interesting to hear him interview the Castelles, and their story had been fascinating. But.

Yeah, *but*. Here she sat listening to an innocuous conversation about the history of this town. How could most of that be involved in a ghost hunt?

Then her interest awoke again.

Steve asked, "Do you know anything about the house at the edge of the town that the Castelles have bought?"

Miss Emma frowned. "I heard a family had moved in, if you mean that farmhouse to the east of here."

"That's it."

"Off Granger Road," Candy elucidated.

Emma nodded thoughtfully. "I'm not specifically aware of the history. I know when I was young it had become the subject of campfire stories. But an empty house is a perfect stage for that."

Steve leaned forward a bit. "It was empty for a long time?"

"Yes, it was," Emma answered. "You'd have to go to the recorder's office to get any details, though. It hasn't been high on my list of things to learn." She smiled slightly. "As a historian, I prefer the broader sweep in the local area. You can get details from the recorder."

"I'll do that. Thank you very much."

Steve was standing when Emma said, "You know who might have more personal information? The previous sheriff, Nate Tate." She looked at Candy. "Have you met him?"

"Not yet, but I've heard plenty about him."

Emma's smile broadened. "He's local icon. You don't want to miss the chance. I'm sure Gage can set it up."

"Gage?" Steve enquired.

"My husband, a.k.a. the current sheriff."

"Wow," Steve said to Candy as they stepped outside. "The previous sheriff. And her husband. Is this place incestuous or what?"

Candy laughed. "Not really, but it's small. The other woman you glimpsed? Nora Madison, the current police chief's wife."

"Okay, then. Don't steal a book."

"Might be wise."

He stopped on the sidewalk. "You know, if I was a historian, I'd want to spend weeks, if not months, interviewing Miss Emma. She sounds like a font of local information. Unfortunately, I have to be more directed."

"I can see that. First, you don't have months. Second, you need to do a TV show."

"Yep. So about this former sheriff…"

She forestalled him. "I'll get in touch for you, set something up if he's willing."

"Thank you."

"What about the Castelles, though? I don't want to make the appointment if you're going to be tied up."

"No," Steve answered. "I wouldn't want that either. I'm going to call the Castelles this evening and set a time. I'll let you know."

Evening. Evening had crept in while they were in the library, and it was dragging into night. Clouds still sailed through the twilight overhead. She wondered if they'd last another day.

Candy watched Steve drive away and felt a bit of relief. It had been a long day for her, never alone, always alert to matters that didn't especially interest her. Guard duty.

Well, not exactly that, but close enough. She reached to snap her jacket, then to head back to the office. The former sheriff had to be next in her sights.

For Steve it had been a productive day. He'd met his clients face-to-face and had been favorably impressed. He'd also gotten a good lead to that guy, Tate, who might be exactly what he needed for his show.

And Emma herself had provided more information: the house had generated tales of haunting. Now he had to find out how long the house had remained empty or if it had ever been renovated, and if so, had the Castelles done it.

While he might not agree with a lot of the explanations in his field, he knew he had to answer for them. It was widely believed that renovating a house could disturb spirits.

He wasn't inclined to believe it. He had a general problem with the whole idea of people hanging around after death. But if they did, why should they get exercised because a house had been altered? Especially since that house had probably been altered more than once over time?

The other problem he had was a simple one: too many ghost hunters spoke for the dead. Unless there was some communication with the so-called spirits, how could anyone know what they were thinking? Assuming they could think at all.

He was a skeptic by nature, but he also accepted his own curiosity about the subject. He'd like to know. Really. He'd like to settle all this in his own mind somehow. So far he hadn't been able to.

That left him with doing his best to reassure frightened people. After he met Viv, and started to build a relationship with her, he was going to go all over that house and property, looking for a rational explanation.

And he was going to explore the family's background. He picked up the phone to call his researcher, Dena.

One thing he knew for sure: if that child was genuinely hearing a man's voice in her room, he was going to get to the bottom of it.

Chapter Four

The next day, Steve awoke refreshed and ready to begin. His hope for conversations with more locals had begun to get answered the evening before at the diner.

Apparently, word was getting around that he was in town to do a TV show. Some folks even recognized him. A few actually stayed to talk after a greeting.

He hadn't gotten any truly useful information, but he felt that might come eventually. It was difficult right now because he didn't want the whole community to know whose house he was investigating. That might hamper his work, but worse, it might upset the Castelles to become front-page news before there'd been a solution.

He got it. They didn't want people all over town discussing whether their daughter had a mental problem or whether they sucked as parents. Who would?

He didn't yet have anything to legitimize their experiences. That was a bad way to go public. The Castelles had every right to expect better of him. It would be different once he had some answers for them, but he didn't need a warning announcement that they wouldn't be happy if they ended up with neighbors camping outside because of curiosity. Or teens being drawn because it was cool there might be a ghost.

Or Viv facing teasing from classmates.

It wouldn't take long for one nightmare to become a second.

He ate breakfast at the truck stop because it was conveniently across the road from the motel. And maybe because it gave him some thinking space to be in a place populated mostly by transients. Nobody here was likely to want to talk to him about much, if anything.

BEN WITTES LEARNED that the guy he'd seen was the ghost hunter. He was delighted with the possibilities. He could speak for the spirits who lingered so unhappily. He called the show's producers to see if they would use him.

The spirits had been clamoring for attention for weeks now, as if they knew who was coming. They surely wanted Ben to speak for them, the voiceless who couldn't begin to speak for themselves.

Ben was the only voice they had, and it made the inside of his head awfully noisy. It's not like he could simply turn them off. Yeah, he could get them to tone it down, but he knew they were desperate. He felt guilty sometimes for not listening more or better.

Lately one voice had become louder than the rest. He wasn't sure who exactly it was, but he kept listening for information.

In the meantime, Ben had a bigger worry. He often woke in the morning with dirt on him, under his nails and on his clothes. Why was he dressed and what was he doing at night? He had no idea, and that frightened him. What if one of the spirits was taking him over?

They had no limits on what they could do, not anymore.

Heaven and hell no longer bound them.

Chapter Five

Steve went over to the Castelles' in the morning to meet Vivian. He left a message on Candy's phone about where he was going and why, but he couldn't imagine any reason for her to want to follow him.

She was a liaison, not a guard, and while he liked to have a connection with the local cops, he didn't need to be constantly watched. It wasn't as if he were any kind of threat to the community.

He met Buddy first. Last night he'd spent some time online looking up the two breeds the Castelles had indicated, wanting to know what he might be getting into with this "big" dog. If they didn't get along, he'd ask to get to know Vivian without her pet. It would be better, however, if she had Buddy with her to relax her and give her a friend at her side.

The dog resembled the American Staffordshire breed more than he looked like a bloodhound, but he had some cute wrinkles on his forehead that seemed to give him character. He was also taller than an Am Staff, closer in size to a bloodhound.

Steve also quickly discovered that Buddy had the bloodhound personality: gentle, sweet, affectionate. It didn't take them long to become fast friends, and

Buddy showed absolutely no hesitation about welcoming Steve. The Castelles had been right about him— he was more likely to knock you over and love you to death.

Buddy also had a bloodhound's nose. When he fixated on an odor, he forgot everything else until he was satisfied.

Which got Steve to thinking about the dog staring at the wall like that. Maybe he hadn't been sensing danger. Maybe there was a smell that had caught his attention.

An interesting change in perspective.

As Steve sat on the grass with the large dog stretched out beside him, content to be scratched until Steve thought his arm might fall off, he thought about Buddy staring fixated at the wall.

There had to be some kind of odor, he decided. Buddy wouldn't stare fixedly at a sound. But what? It could be almost anything. Maybe there was a smell in the wall itself or coming up from the basement. He'd have to check it out.

A good lead for a start. Something other than the obvious paranormal.

Although that didn't do a damn thing to explain the voices Vivian was hearing, or the talking that Annabelle had briefly heard.

Lying back on the cold, hard ground, he stared up at the gray sky while Buddy sniffed him. Okay, maybe it hadn't been an odor that had caught Buddy's attention. He'd heard of dogs reacting to the paranormal, although that was another idea he needed to check out for himself. Maybe Buddy would wind up helping him with that.

At last he sat up, convinced that the dog wouldn't be a problem, and headed into the house to meet with Vivian. While he didn't want anyone to disturb his conversation with the girl, and it would be totally innocuous to start, he didn't want to take the child away with him, not even as far as the backyard, on their first meeting.

He was sure Vivian had been given all the stranger warnings, especially in the big city.

Annabelle and Vivian were sitting in the kitchen. Steve smelled hot chocolate and Vivian had some of it smeared around her mouth. She looked at him rather suspiciously.

Central casting couldn't have sent him a more photogenic child. Long blond wavy hair, bright blue eyes. A pretty child's face.

"Viv," Annabelle said, "this is Mr. Hawks. He's going to try to find out about the voice you keep hearing."

Viv's expression didn't relax very much. He guessed it was a topic she didn't want to visit.

He queried Annabelle with his eyes and joined the two of them at the kitchen table. "You can call me Steve, Vivian," he said pleasantly. "If I get to use your first name, you get to use mine."

That brought a slight smile to Vivian's lips. Annabelle handed her a napkin, and Viv wiped her mouth with it.

Buddy had followed Steve in, and now he sat beside Vivian, looking even larger when measured against the girl's size. That dog had to seriously outweigh her.

"Buddy's a great dog," Steve said. "I like him a whole lot. But he's so big. Does he listen to you?"

Viv nodded, set down her mug, then leaned over

to hug Buddy right around his neck. The dog started grinning.

Okay, Steve thought. That relationship had been established.

"Did you get Buddy when he was a small puppy?"

Vivian answered for the first time. "He's still a puppy."

Annabelle spoke. "I think Steve is asking about when we first got him, when he was still a baby."

And that was why he needed to gain Vivian's trust so he could talk to her alone. Annabelle would mean well, but she'd insert as she thought necessary for clarity. Not what Steve wanted at all.

Vivian was okay with it, however. She let go of Buddy's neck and spread her arms, palms turned inward. "He was this big."

"Not very big at all."

"Smaller than me," Vivian asserted. "He slept in my bed."

"Does he still? I mean, if he sleeps in your bed, where do you sleep?"

That drew a giggle out of the girl. "I make myself tiny."

"I bet you do. Very tiny."

And this added yet another wrinkle. If the dog was sleeping in her room, why was she so scared? Maybe because Buddy wasn't protective? Or did she think Buddy didn't hear the sounds because her parents didn't?

Or, if she thought it was a ghost, nobody else needed to hear it at all?

Or even, from his perspective, voices didn't bother

that dog at all. Given how friendly he was, maybe it was just another background noise to him.

A little over an hour later, Steve departed, promising to return the next day. He'd played card games with Viv, who was on her way to becoming a card sharp. He'd never done so badly with a simple game of War. She had the devil's own luck on a deal.

Vivian's acceptance of him had begun. Good.

Now he needed to find a way to look into the history of the Castelle house. Was there lore associated with it? Was there some kind of notable history?

First place to start was the recorder's office. All the details about who had owned and sold the land back to whenever they started keeping records of such things. Probably pretty decent records since he was sure that the Castelles couldn't have gotten a mortgage without a clear title. The title company would have taken care of that.

When he checked his phone, however, he discovered the nearest title company was ninety miles away…and he couldn't even be sure it was the right one. Chances were the Castelles wouldn't know either. Mortgage companies tended to deal with title companies themselves, keeping the certificate on hand. And charging the client for it, of course.

Sometimes he walked the edge of being cynical. He supposed he was fortunate that after all those years of being a cop he hadn't become hardened and jaded.

He wondered, too, when Candy would get back to him about meeting that retired sheriff. He was already champing at the bit for that interview.

As well as one with Vivian. That child was as smart as a whip, sharp as a tack or whatever overused simile you wanted. He anticipated she'd give him a view that her parents couldn't begin to.

CANDY SPENT MOST of her day trying to track down Nathan Tate for Steve. No answer on the phone, not even his cell, and when she went by the Tate house, no one was home.

Well, people had lives. They weren't all sitting around waiting for a chance to talk to Steve Hawks. Steve was just going to have to do the waiting, and she wasn't about to knock on neighboring doors to find out where the Tates were. Man, imagine the uproar she'd cause. No explanation could ease the fears that would arise from a deputy asking those questions.

Giving up for now, she headed back to the office, believing there had to be something truly useful to do. Not that this department seemed to be overburdened most of the time. If you wanted excitement on a regular basis, this wasn't the place to get it.

Just as she was about to enter, she saw Steve climbing the courthouse steps. The courthouse was located in a large area between four streets that contained a park, as well. It was aptly named Courthouse Square, surrounded on four sides by shops, a bakery and an ice cream parlor. Behind the sheriff's office, facing the square, was a decently sized phone service to help people experiencing everything from abuse to suicidal thoughts.

People everywhere needed someone they could privately talk with, with someone who was objective and could give them advice or get them help.

Diners, like Maude's, weren't the best place to have a personal conversation. Too many ears might overhear.

Instead of going inside, she followed Steve to the courthouse in case she could help. She suspected he was headed for the recorder's office, and she shortly was proved right.

She found him talking to one of the clerks and learning the reality of a truly small town.

"Well, Mr. Hawks, we may have nearly fifty years of records on microfilm and microfiche. I'm not sure about earlier records, or whether any were hit-and-miss. We've got other records over at storage, if you need us to hunt them up."

"I hope I won't," he answered.

The clerk laughed. "I hope so, too. We're a very small department because of budgets, and because we're not all that busy." She lifted an eyebrow. "I think you can tell we aren't having a boom on sales of property, or purchases for that matter."

It was his turn to laugh. "I hope you aren't. A boom would disrupt your town, wouldn't it? It seems so peaceful."

She leaned forward a bit and lowered her voice. "This place is eternally hoping for a boom. At least we got the junior college."

She promised to find the records she could on fiche and film. He thanked her and turned away, spying Candy immediately.

"Riding herd on me?"

She shook her head. "I just couldn't resist seeing how you responded to this reality. We've got the same thing going on over at the sheriff's. Recent records are digitized. Everything's still on paper, though, because we don't want any computer mess-ups."

He laughed. "Gotcha. I hope I won't have to ask anyone to dig into archives."

"It would be greatly appreciated by the men and women who work over at the archive building."

He glanced at the wall clock hanging just behind the recorder's window. "Dang, I knew I was getting hungry. No lunch and it's almost dinnertime. You said Mahoney's is good?"

"Very good with a limited menu. There might even be some people there who'd be willing to talk to you about the Castelle place."

He looked mildly surprised. "But not at Maude's?"

"You might still be under suspicion over there. New fella."

"Why is Mahoney's different?"

"Give anyone a few beers and they're much more likely to talk."

He laughed again. "Come with me?"

He watched her hesitate, then she nodded. "Sure. Maybe my uniform will vouch for you more than a few beers. Of course, it could have a very different effect."

He knew exactly what she meant. When he'd been in uniform, he'd noticed how quiet even a rowdy place could get when he entered.

As they walked down the street, taking in some of the spurt of Halloween decorations in the shop windows, he asked, "People around here don't like to see uniforms?"

"I wouldn't say that. I'm new, too. When some of the other deputies and I drop in after a shift, there's usually a lot of friendliness. I don't see as much if I go in alone."

For the first time he considered how new she was

here, and how that could affect most of her daily life. "It takes a while to get rooted?"

"Probably an entire lifetime." She paused. "I never forget that at least ninety percent of the people here grew up together. This town, this county, is rare."

"These days, yeah. People in other places are a lot more physically mobile."

"I was an Army brat. Funny how close people in the military can get over time. We might change postings, but eventually you run into people you knew from a previous posting. Made it kind of difficult on kids, though."

She paused as they reached the door of Mahoney's. "When my dad was in, changes in postings occurred more frequently than now. Each move was wrenching, mainly because we were kids. You'd make a friend, then move. Next time you ran into them, they'd have changed and I would have changed, too. That meant starting all over again."

She came by her interest in the military honestly. He tucked that away in his mental file. Then he reached for the handle and opened the door. "I hadn't thought about that."

"No reason you should."

Inside the bar was warming up for the evening. Some of the tables were already full. Country music played in the background. There were only a few stools at the bar that remained empty. Steve liked the atmosphere. He wouldn't have been surprised to learn that this bar dated back to the days of the Wild West.

They settled at a table against a wall, and Candy sat facing the door.

A cheerful waitress came over to take their orders,

quite a difference from Maude. Both ordered fried chicken, and Steve asked for a beer while Candy chose club soda with lime.

"Aren't you off duty?" he asked.

"Not right now."

Steve leaned back, wondering if she considered herself on duty because of him, or if she just didn't like to drink. The latter was always possible. It made no difference to him as long as he wasn't hampering her. He didn't know how to ask because it really wasn't his business. Her choice.

He noted again how attractive she was. A beautiful face surrounded by short, dark hair and decorated with warm brown eyes. Eyes that he had seen grow chilly.

Their drinks arrived quickly and were followed soon by the chicken. He suspected this bar turned over chicken swiftly. A quick scan of the people around them suggested he was right. Lots of plates of chicken out there. Well, that boded well.

At least there was no plate of fries to tempt him. He smiled.

"Something funny?" she asked.

"Only me. I was feeling grateful there are no fries."

At last she laughed. "Good point. You're killing my diet."

"Mine, too. Oh, well. A couple of weeks of self-indulgence won't kill me."

"You ever heard that old joke? If I'd known I was going to live this long, I would have taken better care of myself."

"Ha! No, that's the first time. I like it."

A thaw had begun. He felt Candy had let go of a little of her suspicion.

Well, he'd grown used to that ever since he started doing his show. Back when he'd been a cop trying to help frightened families, he'd been more warmly welcomed. It was reasonable for people to question his motives now, although he found it a bit tiresome to keep dealing with it. Maybe someday he'd be treated less like a con man. Although that was improving as his show became better known.

He just wanted people to realize he was honest. Maybe that was the thing that bothered him most. Oh, well, he'd chosen this path and he very much believed in personal responsibility for choices.

Which didn't always make them easier to endure.

They ate silently for a while, and he wondered what he should be talking about. "You get anywhere with the old sheriff?"

Yeah, dude, bright. Bring up work when she should be enjoying dinner. With him, however, questions seldom stopped.

"No luck so far," she answered, looking up from her two pieces of fried chicken. "He's out of town, and I'm damned if I'm going to question neighbors about when he'll be back."

"Afraid of worrying people?"

"Of course I am. How many times did you flash a badge without creating a stir?"

"Rarely," he admitted. "I met Vivian Castelle today."

She nodded and wiped her fingers with a napkin. "How did that go?"

"Pretty well, actually. Bright kid, she opened up some with me after numerous games of War."

"War?"

"A card game that even younger kids can play. She

beat me soundly. I wouldn't want to argue with that child's luck."

That drew a wide smile from her. "Like that?"

"It didn't matter which of us dealt. Anyway, I'll probably need some more time with her before she's ready to talk about her experiences."

"How come?"

"Because I need her to speak for herself without Mom or Dad correcting her or adding things to clarify. I want *her* story."

"Makes sense."

Well, she'd talk about the case, but not about herself it seemed. Silence until that came up. Past bad experience? Or her nature? Whatever the cause, he wanted to find a way around it. To discover something about her.

And maybe that was just a man's response to a woman he found to be beautiful. Or maybe not. Crap. He'd heard women complain that men wanted to talk only about themselves. He didn't want to be that guy. Yet here he was, talking about his job. Every single minute.

So he attacked the problem indirectly. "Still worried I'm taking advantage of people's desperation?"

She paused, halfway through her second chicken thigh. A dark meat lover. "Maybe less than I was since I heard your interview with the Castelles."

"Why's that?"

"Because you never once led them or prompted them. It was all about what they thought and felt."

She'd noticed that. Good. He tried hard not to lead his clients. Another skill of a good detective. Let the witness or suspect tell it. Ask questions, but don't suggest. Suggesting often led to lies that later wouldn't stand up.

She spoke again as she finished her chicken and tried to wipe her fingers and mouth with yet another napkin.

Steve said, "Don't you wish restaurants served those heated finger towels? Or the little bowls of hot water with lemon in them?"

"Oh, yeah, it would be nice. I'll go to the ladies' in a few to wash up. What about your cases?"

No diverting her. Easier than talking about Candy, apparently, he thought as he finished his own meal. "I told you about the cases with people who feared noises in their house, or the feeling that someone was looking in their windows. Or the figures they believed they saw."

She nodded and crumpled the napkin on her plate. The waitress whisked it away and gave her another club soda. "That's a general description."

"It's hard to cover one particularly. Lemme think for a minute or two. See if a case stands out. Do they serve Corona here?"

"They might. Most people just get draft beer."

"I'm fond of Corona." He lifted a finger and the cheerful waitress returned. He wondered if she'd be feeling this perky at closing time. There was little question this bar was going to get rowdier. "Do you have Corona?"

"Oh, yeah. It's become really popular among our younger customers."

"Thanks. Candy, do you want anything?"

"A nice cup of hot chocolate, Mary. Please."

Steve looked wryly at Candy as Mary weaved her

way back toward the bar. "I should have asked about the Corona when I first ordered. But the draft on tap is good."

"I can't tell the difference between one beer and another. Maybe because I drink it so rarely."

"That would matter. Now about my cases when I was still a cop…"

CANDY WAITED PATIENTLY even after her hot chocolate and Steve's longneck arrived. She wanted to hear this, hear what had been important enough to pick up an off-duty avocation. She had begun to think that he was truly concerned about people, but she needed more convincing.

"Well, I remember a case about an elderly lady living alone in a large house. She was *very* old, maybe close to ninety, and frail. Honestly, I couldn't believe she was rattling around in that place all by herself. Still cooking for herself, still cleaning the areas she used. I was impressed, but what if she hurt herself? She didn't even have one of those buttons to call for help, you know the ones that hang around the neck?"

She nodded. "I hear they're not cheap."

"That may have been part of the problem. Social Security doesn't go very far, and she owned the house. That meant upkeep, of course, but I'd have bet she'd socked something away against that. In the meantime, she didn't have rent to pay, and these days that's as expensive as a mortgage."

"Maybe so." Candy could see that. "She was probably very independent, too."

"She also didn't want to leave because that house held more than sixty good years of memories for her.

She talked about her husband, about her children and grandchildren. Even great-grandchildren. It was a short litany, waving at framed photos, but I stood there listening and wondering where all those people were. None of them might be able to talk her out of that house, but surely there was someone who could come stay with her?"

Candy shook her head.

"I know. I don't know where they all were. Families often move away pursuing jobs. I get it. You joined the Army. I'll bet your dad had been out for a while."

"Well, yeah."

"So okay. My parents are retired in Costa Rica. I can't just bop down every weekend to visit. Or every month for that matter. But I *can* hire someone to help them out and check on them."

"Good point." She so far liked the way he thought. Concern for an old woman he didn't really know. Thinking of ways to help his parents. "Anyway..." She pressed him.

"Anyway. I was doing a wellness check, not just answering her call. Back then I was a uniform, so I was pretty sure she felt better having me there. Having my partner, too, although he was outside checking around the house. Which was isolated. Still farmland, although run over by that time. Plenty of brush and woods to hide in, so he had his job cut out for him."

"I can imagine. But one question?"

"Yeah?"

"Were all these places you checked isolated?"

"Nope." He shook his head a little. "Some were in busy neighborhoods. Some people had neighbors who'd had experiences in their houses."

Uneasiness trickled down Candy's spine. Did she really want to hear this? Everyone carried a bit of superstition, even if it was as mild as knocking on wood. Was she about to run into hers?

This time he corralled himself. "Back to my elderly lady. Anyway, she was alone, isolated. Yeah, I was worried about her. I couldn't mistake how frightened she was. I was even concerned that that kind of fear might kill her."

"I didn't think of that, but you're right." Candy frowned. His imagery was vivid.

"If you'd seen her, you'd have shared the same concerns. But back to the rest of it. She kept seeing this black shadow of a man. He'd just suddenly be there, in a doorway or beside her bed. Then he was gone, and she told herself she was imagining it. But when it kept happening, she wondered if she was losing her mind, so she didn't call anyone about it. And then she heard banging and footsteps upstairs. Night after night. She was convinced someone had broken in, and after a week of that, she called us."

"She took it for that long?" Candy was amazed.

"Yeah, I know. But she was afraid for her mind. Afraid someone would come and put her in an institution."

"Rock and a hard place," she murmured. She was building one hell of a picture in her mind and could well understand why Steve would hate leaving her alone. "You didn't call anyone?"

"How could I? She'd made it clear that leaving that house would likely be the death of her. I didn't want to be responsible for that."

Candy put her chin in her hand, forgetting the large

mug of hot chocolate that still steamed in front of her.
"Wow."

"Yeah. Anyway, I searched the entire house for in-
truders. Top to bottom, including a dusty attic. Windows all locked, no sign of forced entry. I had to go
back and tell her there was no one in her house. Then
my partner came in and said he hadn't been able to
find signs of anyone outside, although he did say kids
might have run away too quick to be seen."

"That didn't help, did it?"

Steve sighed. "Not on two levels. First, she hadn't
complained about anyone being outside. Second, even
though everything that was troubling her was indoors,
I couldn't find a damn thing. I told her if she heard or
saw anything more, she must definitely call the emergency line. I told her I'd make sure someone came right
away. I made her promise to call."

His gaze grew distant. "I left feeling like crap, feeling helpless. I got annoyed with my partner for dismiss-
ing it as an old lady all alone and wanting attention. He
even called her batty. I couldn't dismiss it."

He drank some of his beer, then focused on her
again. "I couldn't just toss it for a lot of reasons, and
one of them was I'd been hearing other complaints just
like it. This whole haunting thing was beginning to
trouble me. And that's when it really began."

She remembered her hot chocolate and lifted the
mug. Mahoney's made the best. Rich and creamy. "Did
the woman call again?"

"Two days later. A patrol headed out there as quickly
as they could and found nothing. Again. When I heard
some officers talking about it being a waste of time

and that the woman needed an ambulance, not a cop, I made up my mind I was going out there."

"I would have, too," Candy agreed. "Good for you."

He smiled faintly. "Not within my purview as a cop, but within it off duty. She recognized me and we got going on a complete investigation."

Dang, Candy thought, it was becoming increasingly difficult to distrust this man. He was really too handsome for one thing. Not storybook handsome, but appealing. Now she had to deal with her hormones, as well. Great. Just great.

She thought about the scene he had painted so effectively, mostly thinking about that poor old woman stubbornly living in a house she had loved for many decades, only to find herself terrified inside it. "Did you help her?"

"I don't think so. I went out at night to her house to investigate. I stayed all night as often as my schedule would allow. Several times a week for a few weeks. Never heard anything, never saw anything. Nor did she."

Candy nodded. "So you had to give up?"

"Sort of." He shook his head, looking sad. "I installed cameras in every place she'd had an experience. I put sound-activated recorders in every room. I think they made her feel better, knowing I'd be watching and listening by long distance."

He sighed and put his beer bottle to one side. "Never recorded anything. Then she died a few months later. It'll always be a mystery."

"You don't like that."

"Hell no. Sometimes there's a rational explanation. Sometimes I can at least provide comfort, and sometimes I doubt I give people anything at all. I can only try."

He leaned toward her. "You know what a psychologist told me?"

"What?" She wanted to hear this.

"A lot of his colleagues are seeing a large uptick in patients who come to them with complaints of anxiety, fear and depression. The patients are blaming it on the paranormal. The psychologists are blaming it on the huge number of ghost-hunting shows, and say they spend a lot of time trying to deprogram people."

She felt her eyes widen. "My God. How did that make you feel?"

"Not good. On the other hand, I try to find reasonable explanations, and failing that I try to make people comfortable with what they're experiencing. It's all I can do. Considering the number of people who call for help, I can't ignore the problem."

Candy experienced her first sympathy for him. "Have you ever sent anyone to a psychologist?"

"Hell yeah. I just don't usually do it on screen. Some things need to be kept private. Can we go?"

BEN WITTES WALKED into Mahoney's in time to see that deputy and the ghost hunter leaving. Interesting combination.

One of the damn spirit voices emerged loudly into his head.

Get on with it!

Sure, as if he could just insert himself into that investigation. Just walk up and demand it.

Shut up! he shouted inside his head. *Damn it, just shut up.* He ought to be able to enjoy a sandwich and a beer without being pummeled by annoying spirits.

The voice that had been growing louder and more

demanding quieted down, but the voices in the background became annoying mumbles, mainly because he couldn't make out what they were saying.

He ignored them as best he could. There were a couple of empty stools at the bar and he slid into one. Nobody greeted him, but he was used to that. His entire life in this town people had ignored him. Except for the bullies in school, but even then he'd realized he wasn't the only one being bullied. *Nothing personal in it*, his mother had always said.

However, that one spirit was right. If he could get himself on that ghost-hunting show, he wouldn't be ignored any longer. He *had* to manage it.

For a while it would even make him a big man around here.

That thought was satisfying enough that he smiled at his tuna salad sandwich and tried to figure it out. If the show's producers didn't call him back soon, he'd find another way.

Chapter Six

Candy had plenty to think about that evening. Outside, Halloween was approaching with snow flurries and more carved and lighted pumpkins.

Inside her snug little rental house—*snug* being another word for *tiny*—bright colors greeted her. Given her heritage, she preferred them to the understated, and she wasn't afraid to splash around reds, yellows, greens and electric blues.

She lit her fireplace for the first time since she'd moved here. She didn't want to use it much, being conscious of its inefficiency and the pollutants it emitted, but this one night it didn't seem like a major sin.

And tonight it was comforting, the dance of flickering orange-and-yellow light around her small living room. The warmth, unregulated, sometimes made her hot. Right then, hot felt good.

Steve had given her much to consider, especially that part about what the psychologist told him. She sipped hot cider spiced with a cinnamon stick and turned everything around in her head.

The statement from the psychologist had surprised her, although in retrospect it shouldn't have. Even though she wasn't a fan, she'd been aware of the increasing number of ghost shows on cable channels. Sometimes she had to look hard for something else.

There *did* seem to be a growing interest in conspiracy theories, too. She wondered if the inclination had always been there and was now coming to the forefront. Probably.

She was no fun, she supposed, but she didn't buy into ghosts, aliens, or UFOs. There were enough real threats to worry about. On the other hand, she guessed it might be enjoyable to fall in with a group of similar believers and carry imagination to its wild conclusions.

But ghosts and the paranormal were different. Those ideas actually scared people, and anxiety and fear could make them sick, whether physically or emotionally.

Cripes, there was no real way to think herself through this. She'd simply have to watch and wait for whatever Steve came up with. She just hoped it helped the Castelles.

Sighing, she got herself another mug of hot cider, then settled in to enjoy the fire, the chilly evening and the comforts of home.

For a long time, her only home had been the people in her squad. Friends. Closer than friends, like family. Except nothing could ever enfold her the way her large family's love had. A boisterous crew of immediate family and extended family, aunts, uncles, cousins.

She had walked away to join the Army, an attempt to find herself. A youthful notion, an identity crisis, maybe a need to follow in her deceased father's footsteps. Whatever. But that had carried her to places that had made her unwilling to go home. Changed forever, not wanting her family to know this new person. Maybe not wise, but the feeling ran deep anyway.

Worse, her younger brother had followed her into the Army, and he'd been killed in action. The guilt dogged her constantly. She felt responsible, and she couldn't believe the rest of her family didn't feel the same, at some level. They'd deny it, but she would still know it was true.

With difficulty, she yanked herself away from that yawning cavern before it consumed her. These days it was easy to trip into places inside herself that were hideous.

She sighed again and began listening to some of her favorite songs in her head. It was a skill she'd chosen to develop during many long, tense nights. It was almost as good as having a CD player in her pocket, except it didn't get in the way of her hearing.

Part of her wanted to close her eyes and just let the warmth flow over her. Another part wanted to enjoy the dancing of the firelight.

She kept her eyes open as long as she could and thought about the coming day. This might get exciting.

ON THE OTHER side of town, Steve made some calls to his production crew from his motel room. They'd found a psychic for him, he was told. One right there in Conard City.

Great, he thought, but held his tongue. He'd argued with them about this before and was always told that the fans liked it.

Just because the fans liked it didn't mean he had to. They'd probably like it even more if he ever found proof of a ghost, but it sure as hell was going to take more to convince him than a psychic wandering around claiming to *feel* things. From his perspective, his clients were already feeling enough.

They could do the job themselves. *In this room we feel like something evil is watching. Over there we've seen a black shadow figure. This is horrifying. I believe he wants to hurt my family.*

Well, all the psychic usually did was say the same thing from a different perspective. Which was not to say he was convinced real psychics didn't exist. There'd been a few who'd made the hair on the back of his neck stand up.

But most of them just made him want to roll his eyes.

Having a psychic from right around here was especially problematic. They'd be clued in to the local history, able to repeat stories and anecdotes that would appear to stand up under scrutiny. Except because of Steve's investigation, they rarely would.

He'd seen a few, though, who came in from elsewhere and had no obvious connections with the things they told him, things he had found out independently, and only with a great deal of research. Some of those things weren't available by any means except talking to a local historian. Like Miss Emma.

Come to think of it, he needed to get back to her. Memories might have been spurred by his questions. She might even have done some research of her own to see if she could find something useful.

She'd definitely impressed him. There was an air about her that made her seem both wise and intelligent. He suspected her dismissal of her knowledge of local history had been self-deprecating. She hadn't learned it from growing up surrounded by it. Saying it was her avocation had probably been closer to the truth. A woman like that had to be doing more with her days than simply entering books in a card catalog or checking books out.

Which inevitably led him back to Candy Serrano. She must be bored with this assignment. She was, after all, a woman who'd joined the Army, evidently had seen combat, then had joined a police department. Being a babysitter probably chafed the hell out of her.

He'd heard from a guy at the gas station that Candy's predecessor had been tasked to keep an eye on an angry special ops guy. A paratrooper who was after his brother's killer.

Now here was Candy essentially tasked with the same type of job, only with a much less interesting character. Hell, he was far from being a time bomb ready to blow up.

Nah, he hadn't even been exciting as a detective. Some of his cases, yeah, but not him. It still astonished him to be recognized on the street or in an airport. The low profile he'd once nurtured was in the distant past now.

Well, there didn't seem to be anything to do except embrace it. He'd stepped into this job to help people. He was even able to help people who were never on the show. That was what his spare time was for.

But Candy must be wondering why she'd ever wanted to be a police officer. That was another question he would like her to answer. After a life of such extreme excitement, what was she doing *here*? A charming town to be sure, but maybe too peaceful?

Damn, he wished he could get her to talk about herself. In that regard, she was totally buttoned up.

Then he had a thought. This local psychic. Maybe

she'd have some information about him. Scuttlebutt if nothing else.

He reached for his cell phone and dialed her, wondering if he was going to ruin her evening the way he seemed to be ruining her days.

But he couldn't tolerate inactivity and so far he hadn't accomplished very much. Anything that felt like forward movement would be good.

CANDY HAD DOZED off in her chair but awoke immediately when her phone rang. The fire had died down quite a bit, the room was slowly cooling, but it still felt good. The dancing light had settled to a dull red glow. Nice.

But maybe the phone brought some excitement. She could still use that.

It was Steve, wanting to talk to her about some psychic. She seemed to have a vague memory that there was a guy in town, but she'd had no reason to pursue it. Was he actually going to use a psychic? Her impression of him sank a notch.

She told him to come over and gave him her address. "I've got a fire on the hearth and I don't want to leave it unattended."

"I'll be there shortly."

Whatever it was, she doubted it would be boring. She shook herself out, working out some of the stiffness from sleeping on a recliner, and went to her kitchen to warm up the cider. No beer here. She hoped he'd survive.

BEN WITTES AWOKE in the middle of the night with dirt on his clothes and pine tar sticky on his hands.

What the hell?

He searched his memory and had only a few snatches of having been in the forest. Late evening? He didn't have enough memory to know. Why would he have gone onto the mountainside anyway?

You've got to make it real.

There was that one voice again, louder than the rest. He wished he could silence it by putting the pillow over his ears, but spirits couldn't be shut out by such things.

Staggering wearily, he went to his bathroom and stripped off his dirty clothes. He knew the shower wouldn't get rid of the pine tar, but it would get rid of the dirt he seemed to be wearing all over his hands, and even his legs. Had he been crawling?

As he scrubbed, he noticed pine needles were already beginning to clog the drain. Damn. He wished he knew what was going on.

Stop the deputy.

Stop the deputy from what? Which deputy? The one who was babysitting that ghost hunter? Why would he do that?

Fear had begun to stalk him as he slowly lost control of his nights. What might happen to his days as well if this kept occurring?

Why did he have holes in his memory?

Was he possessed?

The idea of going to the church to ask to be exorcised floated into his brain.

Don't be stupid. The pastor will never believe you. He'll think you're mad.

Ben scraped the pine tar off his hands as best he could, but stronger steps would be needed. He didn't

reach for a towel, for fear of ruining it. Instead he pad-
ded naked and dripping toward his garage.

You're not possessed.

Maybe not yet. And maybe he was well on his way.
His fear deepened. He'd never imagined this.

Possessed.

IT WAS NEARLY midnight when Steve arrived. Candy
smothered a yawn and went to invite him in. Cold
arrived with him, and she regretted not wearing her
sweater.

"Hot cider with cinnamon?" she asked him as he
closed the door behind him.

"You have no idea how good that sounds."

Yeah, she did. That's why she'd been drinking it
herself. "I'll go get it. Have a seat in the living room.
What's left of the fire is warming the space."

"Gladly."

She listened to him walk away as she turned into
her kitchen. Like everything in this house, it was small.
She often wished for more counter space when she got
into a baking or cooking mood. It was, however, bright
with sunflower-yellow paint and blue canisters.

A copper-clad pot on the stove still held warm cider,
and she turned on the gas to heat it up to a better temperature. She wasn't going to look for anything to eat,
though. This wasn't a social visit and Steve wasn't an
invited guest.

It wasn't her mother's way, nor the one she'd been
taught, but Steve didn't qualify even as a friend drop-
ping in. Nope. Her spine had stiffened since leaving
home.

She carried a mug for him and a fresh one for herself

back to the living room. He'd chosen to sit on the sofa rather than her recliner. Maybe because all the stuff on the table beside the recliner labeled it "her" chair.

Mildly amused, she handed him his mug, then sat facing him. "What's up?"

"This cider is really good. And you don't have a TV?"

Strange question. "Not in here. If I watch, it's usually in my bedroom while I'm falling asleep."

"That's so flattering."

She had to grin, deciding she might even enjoy this visit. "Hey, you're not the only one I'm boycotting."

He snorted. "That would make me too important. Anyway, the reason for this terribly rude late-night visit is that my producers have found me a psychic. Not that I want one. I'd rather skip it entirely."

She leaned a little toward him, revising her opinion of him once again. Just a little. "Why? I thought that was part of your genre."

He winced. "For some. I hate it, but the feeling is the fans like it. I don't agree. I mean, I'm running a counter-flow show. Not following the accepted routines or supposed discoveries. I like to think we have a somewhat different fan base. Then the producers pull this."

She nodded. "But doesn't your opinion matter? You're the star."

"It matters less than you'd think. They took a flier on me. Evidently it's working well enough that they keep renewing me. That could end. Or I could quit, I suppose, but that would leave me without a job, and going back to police work wouldn't help me keep my parents in Costa Rica."

She hadn't thought of that. Feeling a bit startled, for

the first time she considered that he was very much in a bind, too.

She asked, "You ever wonder what you'll do if they push you too far in a direction you don't want to go?"

"All the time. Maybe the most important thing to me is my parents. They've dreamed about retiring in Costa Rica since I was in high school. It was less expensive then, and they thought they could make it on Social Security. But over the years, it all grew more expensive, including the income requirements for moving there, and I watched the dream start dying. I was happy as hell to make it possible for them. I absolutely don't want to be the cause of taking it away."

She honestly ached for him. What a tough place to be, with his parents' happiness hanging in the balance. He had to keep his show, and if that meant dealing with psychics, he'd deal.

"Now what about this psychic in town? Do you know anything about him?"

"Just an occasional mention on the grapevine. Nobody seems especially interested, or at least not interested enough to really talk about him."

"Not a superstitious town, huh?"

"I'm not sure I'd say that. Who doesn't knock on wood? Even I do that." She didn't feel sheepish about it either. "Everyone's leery of tempting fate."

"No kidding." Steve sighed. "Nothing? I've wasted your time and kept you awake."

"Not really." Candy sipped more of her cider and considered setting her mug on the hearth to warm it more. It had cooled down fast—everything in a mug did—but she liked it hotter than room temperature. "Anyway, like I was saying, I'm not sure it says anything about superstition. It may just be that this psychic makes them uneasy. I don't know many people who are comfortable with the whole idea of talking to the dead."

"Used to be a big fad, spiritualism." He drained his cup. "Man, that was good. Thanks."

"You're welcome. Anyway, spiritualism. I don't think we've got any table tippers around here. I'd have heard about that by now. No, it just seems to be the one guy, without a following."

"Better for me."

"How's that?"

He smiled crookedly. "I don't have to deal with a bunch of true believers. Which I would, otherwise."

Her turn to smile. Her ignorance about this whole thing was astonishing. Or maybe not, when she'd never been very interested. "I'm taking it that you'd like me to look into this guy? If I can?"

"If he doesn't have some kind of criminal record, I don't know how you could."

"I can ask some of the other deputies what they might have heard. Or my book group at the library. We're meeting next Tuesday."

"That would be a great help. I don't want to go into this blind with this guy if I can manage it."

She had begun to feel kind of achy and breathless. It was as if he had brought an attractant through the door along with the cold air. It seemed to waft around her, drawing her closer to thoughts she didn't want to have.

"I guess I should go and let you get some sleep," Steve said, rising. "Where can I wash this cup?"

"Just leave it. I'll take care of it." She had an urgent need for him to leave before she started down a path that could only get her into trouble. She needed her objectivity, and he was leaving town in a few weeks anyway.

She didn't even walk him to the door. Once he left and she felt as if she could breathe again, she went to lock it.

Now she had to find out about a psychic? Seriously? She hadn't imagined her job this way.

This would mean looking into gossip, too. Oh, well, that could probably be called an official part of her duties. If she didn't listen to the grapevine, she might miss something useful in solving a case.

But a psychic?

Sheesh!

Chapter Seven

Candy walked into the office in the morning. Once again it was unusually silent.

"What's going on?" she asked Sarah Ironheart, who apparently was on the desk today. "Too quiet."

"Yeah. We got a call about a couple of missing teens first thing. Parents say they've been gone since yesterday afternoon, and neither of them is answering their phones. Which isn't necessarily surprising, given how many dead zones we have out here. Probably nothing, but no one's going to take the chance."

"I wouldn't either," Candy agreed. "Want me to run over and get you some coffee? I could do with one. Sleep is still in my eyes."

Sarah smiled almost puckishly. "That would be great. And Velma's not here this morning to be offended."

Candy laughed. "Where is she?"

"Even Velma must occasionally take a day off, like it or not."

"Latte?"

"Oh, that sounds so good!"

Candy strolled down the street to Maude's invigorated by the snap of the clear morning air, enjoying the cardboard Halloween decorations that leered from shop windows.

A couple of teens missing since yesterday afternoon didn't seem like a total all-out emergency. Typical kind of kid stuff, like that vandalism and the toilet papering.

Know where your kids are? Great advice. Try it with teens. They had all kinds of ways to escape parental supervision. Candy knew something about that herself. She had some memories she'd never have shared with her parents on the rare occasion she escaped their constant supervision.

She gave Maude a cheery greeting but had no idea whether it was well received. A couple of minutes later she was headed back to the office with two large take-out cups filled with lattes.

When she arrived to give Sarah her coffee, another deputy was walking around. Micah Parish, a guy who was rumored to be past retirement. He sure didn't look like it. A powerful, Native American man with long, inky hair streaked with silver.

He intimidated her. It was his size that made her wary, even though he'd always been pleasant. A stupid reaction considering where she had been.

"Okay, Sarah," he said, his voice deep, "Where did those extra sat phones go?"

"Gage didn't take them when he left?"

"He wouldn't be asking for them if he had."

"Oh, hell," said Sarah, rising to leave her coffee behind. "Do you suppose grown people ever learn to put things back where they belong?"

Sarah and Micah disappeared to the back, then a short while later she heard Sarah exclaim, "Oh, for heaven's sake!"

"Thanks," Micah answered. "As if I'd ever have looked there!"

"You with all those kids? You'd have gotten around to it."

"Faith saves me the treasure hunts. And those days are pretty much past."

"Not around here."

"Evidently."

A minute later they both reappeared, Micah with a duffel bag that presumably held the missing phones.

Sarah dropped down in her chair, reaching for the coffee and calling out, "See you, Micah."

"Saturday night, right?"

"You betcha."

Candy looked at Sarah. "Saturday?" She knew she had no business asking, but for some reason she couldn't resist.

"Family gathering. I guess you haven't heard, but I'm married to Micah's brother."

That man had a brother? She wondered if the guy was a mountain, too.

Sarah ticked her fingers. "Let's see. My husband, Gideon, is Micah's brother. Connie Parish, whom you know from here, is married to Micah's eldest son, Ethan. There are assorted other Parishes of nearly every age, a few embedded here in this office." Sarah grinned. "Hard to believe that before Micah moved here there were no Parishes at all!"

"But your last name isn't Parish," Candy remarked, completely interested in the abbreviated family tree.

"Ah, well. Gideon's last name is Ironheart. He chose it for himself."

"Is it okay to ask why?"

Sarah shrugged. "No big secret. Gideon and Micah are brothers, but their parents split when they were young. Micah went with his father, and Gideon went with his mother. He's frank about having felt his father abandoned him. They had no contact at all. Then Gideon went to live with his maternal grandfather, where he dug into his mother's Indigenous roots. And there you have it. Ironheart."

Ironheart? It sounded like a good choice for someone who had felt deeply wounded. Almost an aspiration. "That's fascinating, Sarah. Thanks for telling me."

"Why not? Everybody else knows the story. No secrets around here. Anyway, it's a small town and everything gets tangled together sooner or later."

Candy hesitated a moment. "Listen. That ghost-hunter guy I'm tagging after?"

"Steve Hawks. Yeah. What's up?"

"Well, for one thing, he wants to talk with Nathan Tate. Gage gave me the number but I haven't been able to reach Tate."

Sarah nodded. "Hard to do when he and Marge are off visiting their daughter in Los Angeles. He usually turns off his cell."

"Apparently so. A getaway, huh? I'm not in the loop."

Sarah laughed. "You'll be surrounded by the loop soon enough. Give them time. Anyway, Nate should be back in a few days. Anything else?"

"Apparently there's a local psychic."

Sarah frowned faintly. "I've heard a little about him. Ben Wittes. He claims to talk to spirits, I think. True or not, I don't know. What I do know is that most people roll their eyes, which means nothing at all one way or the other. Many of us are dubious."

"I'm not surprised. Steve said he isn't especially thrilled that his producers are thinking about calling the guy in."

At that, Sarah laughed. "I'm not shocked, although I would have expected him to go along."

"He's unexpected in a lot of ways. At the very least, he's not predisposed to believe in the paranormal."

"Now that *is* shocking."

"I thought so, too. Miss Emma said she has his show on DVD. Maybe I should check it out and watch some of it." Candy really didn't want to do that. She wanted her mind clear of any edited preconceptions, and she had no doubt those shows were edited in major ways.

She sighed. "The only other thing I can think of doing is to wait until we talk to Tate, see what he knows about the Castelles' house."

"I agree. If he doesn't know much, I can't imagine where you'd go after that."

Candy rose, tossing her cup into a waste basket. "I'm sure Nate'll have some ideas. Or maybe Steve will."

"Nate likes puzzles, all right. And Hawks has experience. Don't fuss too much, Candy. It's Hawks's problem, not yours."

Good advice, Candy thought as she strolled out onto the street. Excellent advice. Her job was to help and keep him from turning Conard County into a three-ring circus.

Well, the latter was implied, but she figured it was the main reason. She'd been designated the town's protector. Except how she was to do that when she had no control over Steve and his crew? But she absolutely wasn't going to watch his show unless there seemed to be no alternative.

She had her limits, she thought wryly, although she hadn't quite found them yet. Ever.

STEVE EMERGED FROM the truck stop diner, full of pancakes, syrup and bacon. Another sin. Man, he was going to have to make up for a lot when he got home. He was feeling pretty good even so.

Now to hunt up Candy before he went out to talk to Vivian. He believed the Castelles would be more comfortable with Candy there, even though he'd be talking to their daughter alone. They were protective parents, as they should be. He didn't mind that at all. He hoped it wasn't a facade that covered something dark in their background.

He called Candy on her cell. She answered promptly.

"Hey," he said. "Wanna come to the Castelles with me? I think you being there would make them a little more comfortable with me talking to their daughter."

"I guess so," she answered. "Meet you out there."

He'd appreciate it if she didn't sound quite so enthusiastic. On the other hand, he admitted, he wouldn't have been terribly happy in her shoes either.

Well, just get to it. It wasn't as if he'd called on Candy over a stupid matter. Nope. He wouldn't get much out of this town at all if he had to do all this by himself. He knew what he needed, and so far he'd had few enough pointers to the right places and sources. He was, right now, working blind, and he wasn't going to leave that child in a lurch.

SO STEVE WANTED her to lend credibility. Candy felt a bit uneasy about that when she didn't know him very well.

She had seen him be recognized a couple of times, but that didn't help her at all. A TV star hunting for ghosts?

Right. All that meant was that he was who he said he was.

Regardless, she did her duty, arriving at the Castelle house shortly after him. Evidently he'd already gone inside, so she went up and knocked on the door. Annabelle immediately invited her in.

"Good to see you again," Annabelle said with a smile. "Everyone's in the kitchen. Come on and have a hot drink. Coffee, cocoa and tea on tap."

"A warm drink sounds good." It did. It would be a while before she adapted enough to the cold not to want something hot because of the weather.

No sooner had she reached the kitchen and greeted everyone, including a darling girl of about seven, when her radio interrupted.

"Back in a minute," she told the Castelles and Steve. "Gotta take this."

Outside, she keyed in her connection to the office. Sarah answered.

"What's up?" Candy asked.

"We need all hands on deck. We found those kids and it's not good."

Candy raced back into the house and announced briefly, "I have to run. I hope I see you all later."

Then she dashed out again, her stomach knotting, her heart pounding. She couldn't deal with this if it involved a violent crime. She couldn't.

Memories from Afghanistan forced their way up, blistering, searing. Some events had burned their way into her brain, and the scar tissue hadn't thickened.

No, never again.

When she reached the office, deputies swirled around discussing the event and who was going to do what. Gage Dalton commanded.

Sarah motioned her over.

"How bad is it?" Candy asked.

Sarah's face seemed to have frozen in a frown. "They're dead, and from what I've heard, it isn't pretty. We need you here to coordinate traffic. Our dispatcher is going to be overwhelmed for a while."

Candy nodded, feeling relief that she was not being asked to go out to the site. Apparently, someone trusted her to handle communications, new or not. She could do that much and it probably wouldn't rake up any more horrific memories.

Yeah, right. She'd already learned she didn't need imagination to paint savage scenes: the knowledge was already imprinted.

But even though she didn't need to go to the scene, her stomach remained twisted into a painful knot and she began to shake, although not badly. Her heart refused to settle.

It was bad. Already she had too much information.

God, those poor kids, their poor families.

Vivian and her dog seemed comfortable enough. Steve chatted with the Castelles, asking if anything had happened last night.

"Not a thing," Todd answered. "Which isn't helping Viv at all."

Vivian looked up from where she was hugging Buddy.

Steve nodded and smiled at Viv. "I didn't think it

would. I just wanted to know. Are you doing okay, Viv?"

"Not in my bedroom," the girl answered firmly. "I feel safe with Mommy and Daddy, though."

Quite a clear answer. Talking with her should be good. He looked at the Castelles. "Mind if I take Vivian into another room if she's willing?"

Annabelle was the one who bristled a bit. "Why?"

"Because, if she's agreeable, I want to hear the story directly from her. No attempts to clarify, which I can understand you wanting to do. Just let her tell it in her own way."

Todd was standing behind Annabelle and reached out to squeeze her shoulder. "He's right, honey. Her own way in her own time. We'll be nearby."

Annabelle nodded reluctantly.

Steve turned to Vivian. "Viv? You want to talk to me in another room? With Buddy, of course." The dog couldn't amend anything Vivian would say.

"Yes," Viv answered. "Can we play cards, too?"

"Oh, yeah. I've got a deck with me."

Viv smiled. "Okay!"

Then Steve had another question for the Castelles. "I know this isn't a big house, but can we have some privacy?"

Annabelle still looked reluctant, but Todd spoke. "Sure. You don't want her holding back because it's something we don't want to hear. We've got an office. Not much space left after all the stuff we've had to cram in there, but there are two good chairs. Oh, and a tabletop for playing cards."

"Ooh, the office," Vivian said, her blue eyes brightening. She grinned at Steve. "I'm not supposed to go in there."

"Well, this time you can," her father answered. "Just this once. Clear?"

Vivian giggled and jumped off her chair. "Come on, Buddy. Let's show Mr. Steve the office."

The office was pretty much as Todd had described. It was still amazing. He didn't know computer screens came big enough to be large-screen TVs. Large tablets occupied some space and Viv pointed them out proudly. "Daddy sometimes draws me pictures on these and then they're on the TV."

"Wow!"

He saw large posters tacked to the walls that looked like superhero stuff. Keyboards, mice, papers, pencil holders full of colorful pens... The scope of this work must be something else.

Vivian, taking on the role of hostess, placed the two office chairs, one on each side of an empty worktable. Buddy lay down nearby with a small huff. Clearly this wasn't his idea of playtime.

"So why can't you come in here often?" Steve asked casually, although from all the expensive equipment in here he could guess the answer.

"Mommy and Daddy told me I can mess up their work. They said the 'puters are always working even when they're not here. So if I bump something, I could stop the work."

"Makes sense." Her words drew his attention to the background sound of quiet fans blowing. "It's never quiet in here, is it?" Not if these machines never stopped working.

Vivian shook her head and reached for cards as Steve began dealing them. "I like this game."

"I can see why. You always win."

She giggled again. "Mommy says you want to know about my room."

That was direct and to the point. He'd expected to have to draw her slowly into the subject. Cripes, it made her scared enough that she wouldn't go in there anymore, not even to get her toys.

"I do," he answered as they both stacked their cards into neat piles. "What do you most want to tell me?"

"About the man." She kept looking at her cards, her hands steady, but she didn't flip a single card over. She wasn't thinking about them at all. Fear had taken over.

He could have tried to reassure her, but how could he do so truthfully when he didn't know what the hell was happening here?

"The man?" he prompted gently. "Someone you know?"

She shook her head violently. "Bad man. Bad man!"

"That's not good. Tell me what he looks like so I can hunt for him?"

She shook her head. "No. No."

He had to think his way around that. A lot of ways he could respond, none that wouldn't lead her. Damn, he needed to know exactly what *she* experienced.

Then her voice turned almost quiet, even a little singsongy. "I can't talk about him. He might hurt me."

The back of his neck prickled. A break? God, he hoped not. "Viv…"

She lifted her head and her gaze focused on him. Thank God. "Can't see him."

"I can't see him?"

"Nobody can. Not even me."

"Well, that makes it tough. How do you feel about that?"

Vivian swiped the stack of cards away, some of them scattering to the rug. "I don't like it! If Buddy could see him, he'd save me."

Steve looked down at the superfriendly dog and wondered if Viv's certainty about his protectiveness was true. Regardless, he had no doubt that dog could knock a full-grown man off his feet with his relentless friendliness. "Buddy makes you feel safer."

"He used to."

"Used to?"

"He won't come in my room anymore. He used to always sleep with me."

Well, that was downright heartbreaking. "Do you know why he won't come in?"

"The man talks to me. I hate it! But I think Buddy hears it, too, and he hates it, too!" Buddy rose and came to sit right beside her. Some protectiveness there after all. Or concern for Viv's upset.

"It's scarier because you can't see the man?" *Leading. Watch it, Steve.*

"Yeah." Viv quieted and leaned over to wrap her arms around Buddy's neck. The dog visibly leaned into her. "Buddy growled at the wall. Mommy said maybe it was a bug."

"Does he do that often? Growl at the wall?"

Viv held up three fingers as she pressed her face against Buddy.

"Three times, huh?" More than the Castelles had mentioned. But maybe that was three more times when only Vivian had seen it. God. He rubbed his hands over his face. This was going to be a tough one unless he could figure out where that sound was coming from. A radio, a pipe, something being transmitted up through the wall.

But it *could* be as simple as that, so he'd better start hoofing it. He wasn't willing to wait until his crew arrived if he could solve this *now*.

But first, he needed to ask one more question before he let Vivian flee back to her parents.

"Do you know what the man is saying?"

Viv lifted her face and shook her head. "I tried. I told him to shut up."

"Loudly?"

She let go of Buddy. "I screamed it."

"Did it stop?"

"Once."

Steve tucked that one away. He didn't like the pallor that had washed Viv's face while talking about her experience and decided to postpone further questioning. "Come on, let's go back to Mommy and Daddy, okay?"

Viv leaped up as if shot out of her chair and ran back to the kitchen.

Steve wasn't sure how much he had to work with, but he knew one thing for certain: that child wasn't lying. Well, two things. She was also truly terrified.

At the sheriff's office, Candy found little enough to do. The dispatcher, a middle-aged woman named Neesa, handled most of it with the ease of experience. Candy needed to offer her aid only occasionally, mostly to handle standard calls and pass them to deputies and city cops still on patrol.

But then the camera footage began to arrive. Black-and-white, it was being broadcast in as part of the forensics records. Black-and-white or not, Candy mentally filled in the colors and felt her gorge rise.

She didn't want to look, but understood it was expected of her, especially after Gage radioed and told her to keep an eye out for things they might miss, areas that were overlooked.

So she was glued to a view of two older teenagers, one male, one female. Left to die in the night's cold, then presumably savaged by wild animals. She prayed the savaging hadn't come first.

Cruel beyond words. What could those kids possibly have done to deserve this? Nothing. Nobody deserved this. Nobody.

She forced herself to sit in front of the large monitor, doing as she'd been told. Keeping an eye out for blind spots in the camera coverage. Which meant she had to look intently at everything.

"This camera thing is new," Neesa said. "I don't think I like it. Anyway, it's supposed to make sure we don't lose film at the site. Everything gets sent back here and if anything goes black we'll know it before the scene is cleared."

Made sense. Except for people like her who had to sit here and look at the images and couldn't do a damn thing to help.

Then the camera homed in on various wounds. Detailed photos.

Nothing Candy hadn't seen before, but that didn't prevent nausea.

She clicked on the radio and spoke. "So far nothing that remotely resembles knife wounds or gunshot wounds. Mostly tearing wounds."

"Thanks," Gage's gravelly voice came back. "Thought so."

"Well, I'm not a medical examiner."

"None of us are either. I guess we should scan for a weapon anyway. You're going to get close-in shots of the places we look. Have Neesa put it on a split screen. But first I'm going to send you a three-sixty. You catch any jumps, let me know."

"Man, things have changed," Candy muttered. It reminded her of military operations.

"You can thank the commissioners. Gage wanted some more space, to get dispatch into another room because it's hectic and can interfere with comms in both directions."

"Makes sense."

Neesa's response was dry. "Sure. Not to the commissioners. Evidently some new tech caught their eyes. This is what that brings."

"Good backup?" Candy suggested as she watched the screen closely.

"Maybe for the military." Neesa sighed. "Gage is still trying to figure out all the advantages."

"Seems like he's found one."

"Possibly. We'd have gotten all this back on the helmet cams, and from forensics, who are probably already taking over."

Which would be a very good thing, little as she knew about the subject. She almost joined Neesa in a sigh but swallowed it. Bad enough she had to look at this horror.

"Candy?" Gage's voice came through the headset. "You get the full three-sixty?"

"I believe so."

"Okay, we'll let forensics place the markers close to the bodies. We're drawing back to look for anything we might find. Although at this point I think we've scuffed the ground quite a bit."

There was that, she acknowledged. And when this was over, she was probably going to go back to her house and vomit, right up and into dry heaves. Troops on the battlefield often did that, much as civilians might not want to hear it. Few grew hardened enough not to react.

Then there was the so-called thousand-yard stare. The empty, blank look in the eyes when the mind could handle no more. She'd seen that often. Sometimes she'd had it, too. Maybe still did at times.

She wasn't certain she wasn't experiencing it right now, that total shutdown. And she was supposed to go from this back to aiding Steve Hawks. Sure.

STEVE LEFT THE CASTELLES, determined to make a plan of some kind. He needed more info about the house, of course. As he emerged, and was about to climb into his car, he saw a truck pull up at the end of the driveway, blocking it. It might be a friend of the Castelles or someone else, but for a fact he wasn't going anywhere until that truck moved.

He waited, saw the driver climb out. Oh, well, he'd just walk out to meet the guy and ask him to move. He strolled down the drive, his hands tucked in his pockets against the chill. The man, better dressed for the weather but still ragged in appearance, strode toward him, his step a little hesitant.

What was going on here? Someone who didn't know the Castelles after all? Steve felt instantly protective, mainly because of that little girl inside. "Can I help you, stranger?" he asked when they were about six feet apart.

The man paused, stopped walking. "You Steve Hawks? From that ghost show?"

At that moment Steve would have preferred to deny it, but there might be information he needed. "I am."

The man nodded, his gaze growing distant. "I'm Ben Wittes. It's going to happen again."

Steve's attention sharpened. "What is?"

"The murders. Like when Samuel Bride lived here."

Steve felt his insides congeal. "What do you mean?"

"My spirits told me. People will die. The same thing is happening." Wittes looked at him again. "It'll happen again. Don't say I didn't warn you."

Steve, a man who didn't believe in psychics, nonetheless stood frozen as the guy returned to his truck and drove away.

He needed to get to Candy. Maybe that had been a threat.

Or maybe, Steve thought, looking back at the house, this Wittes guy knew something about the Castelles. He still wasn't ready to jump into the perfect-family scenario they painted.

Nobody was that perfect.

Chapter Eight

Candy made it home without puking. It wasn't easy. Her gorge kept trying to rise, but she battled it down and finally reached her kitchen table with a cup of tea, the gentlest thing she could think of. It'd either settle her or get rid of her stomach contents. At this point, even the latter would be a relief. She hadn't even changed out of her uniform, except for ditching her utility belt.

She put her hands on her head and tried not to cry. She had years of experience at holding back tears even though she'd seen plenty of tough guys give in to them occasionally. Still, she had tried not to. Tears might unnerve others who were holding up better.

But there was no one to see her right now, and nothing left to prove. She'd already proved she was as tough as anyone who went into battle. And her life had changed forever.

She couldn't leave it all behind. No way. But with each passing day, she shoved it back deeper into the mental locker.

Until today. She'd seen even more gruesome things, but those kids...

What had they done? Nothing. Nothing at all. Nothing to deserve that. And she hadn't expected to see such graphic video.

That had been a sideways punch to the gut. Maybe she ought to quit and find a different job. Except she'd tried that without success. Unless she wanted to be a mercenary.

Never.

Tears finally started rolling down her cheeks as memories of her time in the Army rolled through her mind. The sound, the smells, the screams. Oh, God, the screams. People she knew torn up, burned, dead. Faces she would never forget, not until the day she died.

Initially, she didn't hear the knock on the door. Eventually it penetrated as it grew louder.

She shook her head, dashed away her tears on her shirtsleeve, hoping there hadn't been another emergency. She'd turned off her radio. She was off duty now, her cell phone was off, and she sure as hell didn't want to be bothered by anything less than a mass shooting in town.

So much for her idea that a small town would be calmer. Less violent. Stupid idea. People were the same everywhere.

She opened the door reluctantly and saw Steve Hawks. "Now's not a good time," she told him. Rudely, but it was the truth.

"I heard," he said. "I heard something."

For some reason that made her step back and let him in. He'd heard what? From where? She doubted the news was making the rounds in town yet. The sheriff had locked down all information. Did that matter? Maybe not, but Steve sure hadn't seen what she'd seen.

"You don't look good," he said as soon as he was inside.

"Tough."

"I'd have brought a bottle if I'd known. You're white. Your eyes are red and swollen. Get your butt into the kitchen and tell me what you can stomach."

He surprised her by reaching out to touch her cheek. "Cold as ice. Where's a blanket?"

What did she care?

Then he spied the throw over the back of the couch in the next room. "Here or the kitchen?"

She moved toward the kitchen. It wasn't as comfortable, but she didn't care about comfort.

When she sat at the table, he spread the throw over her and tucked it around her. Vaguely she sensed the warmth.

"What have you got? Anything you prefer?"

Her lips felt frozen.

"Alrighty, then. I'll look." Followed by, "Damn, I can tell you were in the Army. Remind me to ask you to organize me someday."

Distantly she felt as if that might be amusing. At another time. Right now it seemed pointless. Empty conversation.

Clatters. Cupboard doors closing. Even in this state, situational awareness never deserted her.

"Here." A cup appeared before her. Steam rose from it. She saw it and didn't care.

"Drink," he ordered. "Hot milk."

Hot milk? Her mother had made that for her. "I don't like it."

"Who cares. It'll warm you, maybe help you relax a bit."

Obediently, because she always followed orders, she reached for the mug with trembling hands. Hands that felt as if they belonged to someone else.

She hadn't raised it more than an inch when it slipped from her grip and spilled everywhere. She stared at the milk running across the table, some of it down her front. What did it matter?

She watched Steve's hands and arms as he wiped up the mess, including the milk that had run down her front.

"Okay, that's not going to work. Not until your fingers warm up."

He pulled a chair close and reached for her hands, chafing them with his bigger, warmer ones.

"Come back to me, Candy," he said quietly. "You've come back from far worse."

Had she? Apparently not. Like a tar pit, it just kept bubbling up and dragging her in.

But as he rubbed her hands, she began to return from the nightmare. His gentleness called to her. Drew her back from the brink. Offered her a touch of emotional safety. No one had ever treated her so kindly when the ugliness rose from the pit.

His touch reached her in a way that little enough had. Slowly she drew her hands back and tugged the throw tighter around her.

And gradually her vision returned from the tunnel. She saw Steve, saw her kitchen, saw the rag he'd used to wipe up her mess. Sour milk, she thought irrelevantly. She needed to wash it soon.

"Candy?"

Her gaze trailed back to Steve. "I'm here."

"That was rough for you. Take your time. About that hot drink?"

Her stomach had settled, she realized. "Cider. Please."

"Coming up. I think I'll join you. I'm wondering how any little kids could possibly want to trick-or-treat around here, as cold as it's getting."

"There's an annual Halloween party over at the high school. Or so I've heard."

"Good idea."

More clattering of pans followed by the *glug* of cider pouring from the gallon jug. A short while later, the aroma of hot cider and cinnamon. This time when he put a mug in front of her, she was able to reach with a steadier hand and stir it with the cinnamon stick.

Steve returned to his seat, moving it back to a more respectful distance. He had a mug of his own.

"Whatever you did after you left the Castelles was awful, wasn't it?"

She responded with a jerky nod. "I...didn't have to go to the scene, but the video was being broadcast into the office, and Gage asked me to watch it in case I noticed anything."

"What happened?"

She looked down. "An ugly violent crime." She couldn't say more, not yet.

"God!"

She felt the cider had cooled enough to drink safely, and lifted the mug to her lips, glad to see her hands were steady and her fingers were feeling again. Hot and good. Very good.

She sensed he was withholding something, but she didn't want to deal with it yet. She needed time to put all the tumbled blocks inside her head back into order. Whatever order they might find again.

Steve spoke. "I'm so sorry you had to see that."

"I've seen worse." Which was true. "It's just so pointless. Not combatants. No threat to anyone."

He nodded and reached out to touch her hand briefly. "Take your time. No rush."

But another thought began to penetrate the fog in her head. "You must have come here for a reason."

"Nothing that can't wait until later."

But she could tell he was troubled. For a detective who must have had a poker face at one time, he could be quite transparent. "What's wrong?"

"Nothing exactly. Nothing that can't wait. Not urgent."

She had to live with that, she supposed, at least for a little longer. Steve had a mulish look for the first time since she'd met him. Probably little budged him until he was ready.

A good trait for a detective? Another thing that didn't matter.

She was searching for inanities, she realized. Anything to redirect her own mind. An escape hatch, or a temporary break. Anything that would help her finish moving from the past to the present—and the present wasn't looking especially good right now.

She continued drinking the cider, beginning to wonder if she needed something sweeter. She might be having delayed shock, a mix of today's events with memories.

Something sweet truly sounded good, and for once in her life she didn't mind asking for some help. "On the counter there's a bakery box. Cinnamon rolls. I need one. Please."

"Coming right up. I may join you. Dinner wasn't on my list this afternoon."

"Help yourself."

He found two small plates and brought the rolls to the table. "Maybe someone will eventually explain to me why cinnamon rolls are good for breakfast but not for dinner. Cake is for a dinner dessert, but not for breakfast. Why?"

That cracked the ice that encased her and drew forth a small laugh. "I never thought about it."

"I mean, really, a sweet is a sweet and it shouldn't be rigidly prescribed for a certain meal. I like pie. I'd eat apple pie and peach cobbler for breakfast. But no. I'm welcome to pancakes covered in maple syrup."

"But not for dinner."

"In theory, although I think some restaurants make a good living by providing them round the clock."

"Which ought to tell us something." She had begun to feel grounded again, firmly planted in the present, although that did not banish the murders of those teens. Nothing ever would. Her mind was like that camera she'd spent hours looking at. Odd how you'd forget things you didn't want to and couldn't forget things you wished you could erase forever.

But as she ate the roll and calories began to rush through her system, she remembered something else. "What did you mean, when you said you'd heard something?"

"I was given a vague prediction by this guy claiming to be a psychic. He came to the Castelles', looking for me I think, and told me his spirits had told him that murders were going to happen again. He said it would happen the same way it had when some guy named Bride lived there."

"God!" She dropped the remains of the roll and clenched her hands into fists. "God, Steve! You're a detective. How could you have thought this could wait?"

"Because I didn't know it had happened! I took it as a prediction, probably worthless, and came to you."

But Candy was having none of it. She grabbed the landline phone off the wall and dialed the sheriff's home number.

"Gage, Ben Wittes told Steve Hawks today that people might be murdered."

TWENTY MINUTES LATER, Gage Dalton arrived at Candy's house. He looked slightly rumpled, especially his shirt, as if he had grabbed one from the laundry where he had tossed it.

Steve noticed his appearance. It was hard not to. One side of his face was scarred with burns, and his voice was roughened. There was a story there that Steve decided to ask about later. That detective that Candy had criticized as falling down on the job? He was still detective enough to want to know the stories of people he met.

"Okay," Gage said. "Explain what Ben Wittes said."

Candy waved at him and Steve took over. "It's not much. Ben Wittes showed up at the house I'm investigating. He wanted to tell me one thing. He said his spirits were warning him that the murders were going to begin again, just like they had when a guy named Bride owned the house. I still haven't heard anything about this Bride guy."

Gage frowned. "I seem to vaguely remember something about a guy with that name after I started working for the department. Nothing important, some kind of local story or other. Since it didn't involve me or the department, and was kind of vague anyway, I didn't pay any attention."

"Understandable," Steve replied. "But Candy thought I was a jerk for not reporting it immediately. Former detective and all that."

Gage smiled faintly. "You didn't know what we found today, and the info you got was kind of squirrely anyway."

Steve grinned back. "Hey, I like squirrels. Some of the most intelligent and cute members of the animal kingdom."

Gage shook his head. "Tell that to the folks who spend a lot of time growing gardens only to see them ravaged by these so-called vermin. I think they're a little upset they can't shoot a gun anywhere in town, and they're not allowed to poison anything. Kids and dogs, you know. Or cats."

"I get it," Steve answered. He also liked Gage's answer. People in a tug-of-war against animals just trying to survive. A perennial problem.

But Gage was already rising. "I'm going to bring Wittes in for questioning. You want to be there, Candy?"

"Not tonight."

Gage nodded. "After today I'm not surprised. Must have been hard on you. I wouldn't have asked if I didn't think it was important."

"If you never ask anything of me, you might as well fire me."

Gage paused to pat her shoulder. "You're doing great. With time you'll like the work even more. It's not like we have problems like this very often. Anyway, I'll bring Wittes in tomorrow morning. I'd like you to see his reaction."

Candy nodded. "I'm sure I can do that."

"No rush anyway since this guy claims he's talking to spirits. He won't ßexpect that to change matters so quickly for him, not even if he really knows something."

Then Gage left. Steve didn't move. He wasn't going to leave Candy alone while she was still so fragile emotionally.

She didn't speak for a while, intently staring at the table. He could only imagine the memories this had reawakened in her, but he had some experiences of his own. Well, more than a few. He didn't miss that about his former job. Not one bit.

He rose eventually, deciding she probably needed more calories. He guessed she hadn't been able to eat a thing since she'd been called in to monitor the video.

Overall, a good thing for the sheriff to have. He himself had seen too many blanks from crime scene techs' cameras, from body cams. Everyone seemed to have their own point of view about what was important at the scene.

This time he looked for something in her refrigerator and cupboards that would give her more than a cinnamon roll.

He discovered chicken soup, one of the richer brands, and started with that. If she could get that down, he'd try a sandwich. She had peanut butter on the shelf. He believed he had spied some cold cuts in the lowest drawer of the fridge. Sandwich makings.

He heated the soup in her microwave, then set it before her on the table with a spoon. "Eat."

She hesitated only a few moments before picking up the spoon. "You don't have to babysit me."

"I'm sure. I'm also equally certain that I want to. Quit objecting and get some more food in you."

"What about you?"

"I'll find something after you eat that soup."

He sat waiting, and finally the spoon started making its way between the bowl and her mouth. She reached for a napkin from the basket on the far end of the table and wiped her chin, and he laughed.

"What's so funny?" She looked right at him, a good sign.

"I see we both have a soup-drinking problem. I swear there's a hole in my bottom lip."

She managed a chuckle and went back to her soup. It must have agreed with her because she began to eat faster. That made him feel a whole lot better.

"It's stupid," she said as she finished the soup.

"What is?"

"I've seen things so much worse than those victims. Far worse. I shouldn't have reacted so strongly."

"I don't know about that. Sometimes small things can be enough. A sight, a sound, a smell."

She raised her head from the bowl. "You have it, too?"

"Believe it. While I'm sure my police experiences couldn't be as bad as yours, cases still haunt me."

She clearly pondered that. He rose. "What else can

I feed you? Chicken soup may be great for viral infections, but not so much for shock. Sandwich?"

"There's some sliced ham and some salami in the refrigerator meat drawer. And some Jarlsburg cheese on the next drawer up. Help yourself."

Steve opened the refrigerator again and spied a bottle on the door. "Ooh, you like spicy mustard. A woman after my own heart."

"No other kind," she agreed listlessly.

She was sinking again. Steve found two plates and made some simple ham sandwiches on rye, faster than he'd ever made them before. He needed to get back quickly before the depression snagged her again.

"Here," he said, sitting across from her and placing two plates on the table. "Have at it."

"Thank you."

She still sounded too quiet, too slow. He wondered whether he should bring the subject up now or wait until she'd eaten. Afterward, he decided.

She ate at least. No hesitation this time. Even if her mind was trying to wander elsewhere, her physical needs were taking priority.

When they were both done, he pushed the plates aside. "I want to talk."

She had a distant look in her eyes. He recognized it. "Say, try to come back for just a minute. You don't want to go there."

"No." She drew a deep breath. "Sometimes it's hard."

"I know it is. Are you getting any help with your PTSD?"

Her head jerked. "Why would I? Everyone has bad memories."

"Not the same. Not when they take over like this and give you a thousand-yard stare. Talk to me, Candy. Talk us both through this."

She sighed, picking up her napkin and folding it repeatedly, ignoring the yellow spot of mustard. As if she didn't care about it getting onto her fingers. Right then, she probably didn't.

"Candy? Look at me. Talk to me. Please."

"I'm sorry. I'm not a good conversationalist right now."

"I'm not asking you to make conversation. Just ramble." He was starting to get seriously concerned about her. Maybe it was ER time.

After a minute or so, she sighed. "I ought to be in control."

He waited to see if she would say more. When she didn't, he asked, "In control of what?"

"These memories. The way they take over. When it starts, they just take over. I try to cram them away, but they don't want to stop."

He nodded understanding. "That happens to me occasionally. And you had a massive trigger today. I believe if I'd seen what you watched, I'd probably be having some awful memories, too."

She sighed again and looked up from the napkin, which right now was about an inch square. "Sorry."

"For what? Don't apologize. This is a very difficult thing to deal with. Hell, I don't like to admit I have a problem and I seriously believe mine couldn't possibly be as bad as yours. You've seen a lot more of hell than I have."

She looked away briefly. "Don't minimize your experience, Steve."

"Why the devil not? You're busy minimizing yours. Guess you gotta be tough, huh?"

She looked so sad in that moment that he feared she was about to withdraw. His chest was already so tight with worry and concern that he doubted he could handle that. He was sure she wouldn't like being bundled into the car and taken against her will to the ER. He knew he wouldn't like it.

But then she spoke. "You're right. Be tough. I had to be for so long. I hate to admit any weakness."

"The good old Army. Well, cops have a bit of that, too. To some degree. And sometimes it makes us stupid."

Her gaze snapped right back. Oh, she was here now. Relief nearly swamped him. "Stupid. Are you saying I need treatment?"

"It might help, but that's not my decision. Anyway, I'll sit here all night driving you nuts until you get past this. Wanna play Hearts? Or Spades?"

She shook her head, but a faint smile dawned on her lips. "I never thought you'd become a friend. Is this what you do with your clients?"

"I'm not doing anything except being myself."

Candy chewed her lower lip, then said, "I believe that."

Well, that was good, because he sure as heck wasn't trying to shine her on.

"I think I can go to bed now," she said soon.

"Good. Point me to the couch, because I'm not going anywhere."

At least she didn't argue. She told him where to find spare blankets and a pillow. "You're not going to be comfortable. You're kinda long."

He flashed a smile. "I'll be fine. You get to bed. Morning at the office, yeah?"

"Yeah." Then she rose and walked away.

It still wasn't good, but it was better. At least he knew he'd hear her if she stirred during the night. He'd always slept like a cat.

Chapter Nine

In the morning, Candy felt a whole lot better. She was even eager to talk with Gage. Plus, she'd found a text message from the old sheriff. She told Steve.

"Nate Tate will be back today. He said he'd be glad to see you this evening."

"Well, super!" Steve looked cheerful this morning, as if he was glad to see her back to stability.

She felt embarrassed about last night, but she also felt grateful to him for sticking this out. Maybe she ought to join that veterans group that met on Saturday mornings. As her job would allow. Since those vets kept attending, there must be something useful in it, other than raking up bad memories. She could at least try.

Another beautiful, sunny day greeted her, but it had grown significantly colder. Steve was right. If this kept up, most parents were going to be dragging kids to the Halloween party. Not even that momentous day deserved frostbitten fingertips and noses.

The light snowfall they'd had had disappeared in yesterday's sunshine. Everything was starting to look brown, and the remaining colorful leaves had fallen from the trees.

She still enjoyed the dry air, though, and the sun warmed her anyway. Halloween decorations were blooming like autumn flowers as people added more to their yards and windows. She was feeling pretty good by the time she reached the office. Last night had been firmly shoved into its box, deep in the depths of her brain.

Steve had been wonderful, she thought as she rounded the courthouse square to the office door. Patient, kind, understanding. He was right about her getting some help. If there was anything that could reduce her memories of the nightmare that had been her life for too long, she was willing.

Her fault, however, for not realizing the totality of the problem. Nearly every veteran had some of these experiences, and she'd probably been foolish to believe almost everyone just dealt with it. Foolish to believe her situation was not that bad.

Yesterday had certainly taught her otherwise. She couldn't keep responding so dramatically to these things, not if she wanted to continue life as a cop.

And she did want to continue. She'd been feeling that she'd found a useful purpose at last, one that made her feel good about herself. Yeah, she had to do whatever she could to hang on to this.

Besides, she was growing to love this area, this town.

Feeling reasonably cheerful, she entered the office to face questioning Ben Wittes. That wouldn't be so bad, even if they had reason to believe he might have perpetrated the horrific crime against those teens.

Velma was back at her post at the dispatch desk, smoking her illegal cloud as if laws weren't made for her. Even Gage didn't think it was all that awful, but what was he going to do? Fire a woman who had been part of this department for more years than Candy had been alive? She could easily imagine department staff, including deputies, holding an insurrection.

Velma spoke even before the other deputies greeted her. Sarah Ironheart, Guy Redwing, Beau Beauregard. Friendly, familiar faces now.

But Velma had a message. "Gage wants you to meet him in the interrogation room."

Candy felt a moment of tension. Maybe she wasn't ready for this yet? It didn't matter. She needed to do this.

It had initially surprised her how much the corridors and offices wended through the large building in which they were housed. Apparently the office had snagged a whole bunch of space in the interior, behind the store-fronts that ringed the block. From the street you'd never guess just how much resided inside.

Gage was waiting in the interrogation room, behind a steel table that supported shackle attachment rings on the other side from him. Two chairs sat on each side of the table.

"Ben Wittes should be here soon," he remarked as he motioned her to the chair beside him. "You don't have to question him unless something occurs to you. Just watch his reactions. It's always good to have a second pair of eyes."

"It sure is," she agreed as she took her seat.

"You had any coffee this morning?"

"Only a cup of what I made at home."

He flashed a grin. "I'll get someone else to risk Velma's wrath. Yeah, I'm a chicken when it comes to her. If you haven't noticed, she can breathe fire. You know. Like a dragon."

She laughed. "I've begun to discover that."

"So what'll it be? Black? Strong?"

"Latte, if you don't mind. Maude makes a darn good one."

Gage nodded. "When it comes to cooking, Maude never settles for second best."

He rose and went to open the door. "Hey, Guy? Two coffees. One a tall and black, the other a tall latte."

"Got it, boss." Redwing's voice floated from the front.

"Now," Gage said as he returned to his seat, "if Velma has a problem with that, she can squawk at Guy."

Another bubble of amusement rose in Candy. "What's with this coffee thing? I keep getting the feeling there's some kind of tradition?"

"There is. Velma makes a huge urn full of coffee every time she comes to work. It's famously bad. Only desperation on a busy shift causes anyone to drink it. You must have noticed all the bottles of antacids sitting out near the mugs. That's why."

"But she doesn't notice?"

"If she has, she probably thinks it isn't related to the coffee. It's one of her ways of taking care of us. She has a lot of those, you'll find with time. The department's mom. Who the hell is going to tell her that her coffee sucks?"

Candy understood perfectly. It was just another one of those things that was causing her to like this town.

Guy delivered the coffee just before Ben Wittes walked in, a deputy accompanying him. He looked

"4 for 4" MINI-SURVEY

We are prepared to **REWARD** you with 4 FREE Books and Free Gifts for completing our MINI SURVEY!

Suspenseful Romance

Suspense

You'll get up to...

4 FREE BOOKS & FREE GIFTS

st for participating in our Mini Survey!

Get Up To 4 Free Books!

Dear Reader,

IT'S A FACT: if you answer 4 quick questions, we'll send you 4 FREE REWARDS from each series you try!

Try **Harlequin® Romantic Suspense** books featuring heart-racing page-turners with unexpected plot twists and irresistible chemistry that will keep you guessing to the very end.

Try **Harlequin Intrigue® Larger-Print** books featuring action-packed stories that will keep you on the edge of your seat. Solve the crime and deliver justice at all costs.

Or **TRY BOTH!**

I'm not kidding you. As a leading publisher of women's fiction, we value your opinions... and your time. That's why we are prepared to reward you handsomely for completing our mini-survey. In fact, we have 4 Free Rewards for you, including 2 free books and 2 free gifts from each series you try!

Thank you for participating in our survey,

Pam Powers

www.ReaderService.com

To get your 4 FREE REWARDS:
Complete the survey below and return the insert today to receive up to 4 FREE BOOKS and FREE GIFTS guaranteed!

"4 for 4" MINI-SURVEY

1 Is reading one of your favorite hobbies?
☐ YES ☐ NO

2 Do you prefer to read instead of watch TV?
☐ YES ☐ NO

3 Do you read newspapers and magazines?
☐ YES ☐ NO

4 Do you enjoy trying new book series with FREE BOOKS?
☐ YES ☐ NO

Please send me my Free Rewards, consisting of **2 Free Books from each series I select** and **Free Mystery Gifts**. I understand that I am under no obligation to buy anything, as explained on the back of this card.

☐ **Harlequin® Romantic Suspense** (240/340 HDL GQ5A)
☐ **Harlequin Intrigue® Larger-Print** (199/399 HDL GQ5A)
☐ **Try Both** (240/340 & 199/399 HDL GQ5M)

FIRST NAME   LAST NAME

ADDRESS

APT.#   CITY

STATE/PROV.   ZIP/POSTAL CODE

EMAIL ☐ Please check this box if you would like to receive newsletters and promotional emails from Harlequin Enterprises ULC and its affiliates. You can unsubscribe anytime.

HI/HRS-520-MS20

HARLEQUIN READER SERVICE—Here's how it works:

Accepting your 2 free books and 2 free gifts (gifts valued at approximately $10.00 retail) places you under no obligation to buy anything. You may keep the books and gifts and return the shipping statement marked "cancel." If you do not cancel, approximately one month later we'll send you more books from the series you have chosen, and bill you at our low, subscribers-only discount price. Harlequin® Romantic Suspense books consist of 4 books each month and cost just $4.99 each in the U.S. or $5.74 each in Canada, a savings of at least 13% off the cover price. Harlequin Intrigue® Larger-Print books consist of 6 books each month and cost just $5.99 each for in the U.S. or $6.49 each in Canada, a savings of at least 14% off the cover price. It's quite a bargain! Shipping and handling is just 50¢ per book in the U.S. and $1.25 per book in Canada*. You may return any shipment at our expense and cancel at any time — or you may continue to receive monthly shipments at our low, subscribers-only discount price plus shipping and handling. *Terms and prices subject to change without notice. Prices do not include sales taxes which will be charged (if applicable) based on your state or country of residence. Canadian residents will be charged applicable taxes. Offer not valid in Quebec. Books received may not be as shown. All orders subject to approval. Credit or debit balances in a customer's account(s) may be offset by any other outstanding balance owed by or to the customer. Please allow 3 to 4 weeks for delivery. Offer available while quantities last.

▲ If offer card is missing write to: Harlequin Reader Service, P.O. Box 1341, Buffalo, NY 14240-8531 or visit www.ReaderService.com ▲

BUSINESS REPLY MAIL

FIRST-CLASS MAIL   PERMIT NO. 717   BUFFALO, NY

POSTAGE WILL BE PAID BY ADDRESSEE

HARLEQUIN READER SERVICE

PO BOX 1341

BUFFALO NY 14240-8571

NO POSTAGE
NECESSARY
IF MAILED
IN THE
UNITED STATES

a little surprised to be there, but not at all worried about it.

Candy studied the rather seedy-looking man. Nothing about him appeared to want to draw attention.

Gage greeted him pleasantly and invited him to sit. Ben did, then looked around before shrugging. "I never expected to be here."

"I'm sure you never did," Gage answered. "Nothing to worry about. We just need to ask a couple of questions."

Ben nodded. "What can I do?"

Gage gestured and the other deputy left the room. Candy never doubted that the cameras in the four high corners were recording this interview.

"I was wondering," Gage said, "if you'd heard anything about the murders of two teens on the mountain. You hear a lot."

Not even an Oscar-winning performance could have drained that guy's face so instantly white. He was shocked.

It took Ben a full minute to reply, and by then he had started shaking. "No," he answered unsteadily. "Oh, God, no. I tried to warn that Hawks guy. My spirits said it was going to happen. I never thought…" He trailed off, still visibly shaken. "Oh, my God."

"Your spirits told you?"

Ben nodded. "They never shut up, but lately one voice is getting stronger. My guide, I think. But I never imagined his warning was late."

"So why'd you tell Hawks?"

There was a cup of water on the table, and Ben reached for it, looking at Gage. Receiving a nod, he gulped it all down.

Another few seconds before Ben replied. "I don't always trust my voices. Because nobody believes me when I tell them what I hear. Because Hawks hunts ghosts. I thought he might listen."

For the first time Ben's color changed, growing faintly red. "Because I'm trying to get on his show."

"Ah," Gage replied.

"Is that so awful?"

"Of course not," Candy said soothingly. "A lot of people want to do that." But by now she was convinced this man had no part in the murders. That initial shock could not have been feigned.

Gage spoke. "I guess maybe we should listen to what you have to say more often. Did the spirit tell you anything else?"

"Only that it was beginning again. Like back when Bride owned the house. A long, long time ago."

"Will there be more?"

"I don't know." Ben was beginning to sound almost desperate. "He hasn't said. But if he does, should I tell you?"

"Please," Gage said. "I'll listen. Promise."

Ben left a minute later, clearly immensely relieved. Gage looked at Candy.

"What do you think?"

Candy never hesitated. "Have you ever seen a man turn that white when he heard what had happened? I don't think he did it."

"I'm inclined to agree. That's a color I only see on family members when I bring the bad news. Interesting about his spirit, though."

Candy shifted uncomfortably. "I'm not a believer."

"I haven't been, but maybe I should at least listen."

"Steve was right, though. In and of itself, it didn't matter. And given that neither of them knew about the murders at the time, it makes even more sense not to take it seriously."

"I certainly wouldn't make too much of it. Well, get back to the task I'm sure you love." He winked. "Someone has to be on the bottom rung."

A good way of putting it, Candy thought as she exited the office with most of her latte. Dang that coffee was a perk and it was still hot enough.

She decided, however, in the pursuit of her duties, to follow Steve to the library. It'd be interesting to learn if Miss Emma had come up with anything. Right now, from his perspective, other than the little girl's complaints, the house must seem sterile.

She still wasn't ready to deal with the Ben Wittes thing, however. Gage was right to be willing to listen to him, but the whole idea that this guy was hearing voices in his head and that they might be right gave her the creeps.

Another thing to stash in her hurt locker unless it became important.

She dumped her cup in the bin out front of the library, which clearly stated that no drinks or food were allowed inside.

Steve was inside Emma's office with the door open. Emma spied her and waved her inside.

"We were just talking about the only Bride I can find," Emma said as Candy sat. "Very little in the library about him. A death notice, heart attack. No one at his funeral. His wife had left him twenty years before. In all, sad but unexceptional at this point. I can keep digging, though. You'd be surprised how many things get cross-referenced in the strangest ways."

Outside, Candy and Steve stood on the steps while October's gentle winds chilled them more.

Steve spoke into the biting air. "I said I'd come to the Castelles' house at about two. That leaves some time for Maude's."

She thought about it. Lunch was going to sound good before long and she'd have to take him over to see Nathan Tate this evening. "Let's do it," she answered. "But I pay for my own."

He grinned. "Lunch at Maude's as bribery? It doesn't cost that much."

"Around here, most folks *would* consider it bribery. I left my patrol car at the station, so I'll meet you there."

"You can ride with me, you know. It's part of your job."

She decided he was right. And rarely was there a time when Maude's didn't sound good.

When they walked inside, some of the breakfast crowd were still lingering over their bottomless coffee, but some of the local lunch crowd had begun to arrive. The place was beginning to buzz, and faces were a little friendlier. Steve had crossed the first frontier: he was now known.

Candy felt in luck. Maude had added potato and leek soup to her menu and had apparently gotten into the mood to fry a bunch of chicken. She and Steve ordered both.

"Was Miss Emma a lot of help?" Candy asked.

"She was, considering how long ago this was and how few public records seem to exist."

"We weren't far away from the Wild West then, from what I understand. Records may have been sketchy."

"Miss Emma thinks so. Man, this soup is wonderful."

Candy returned to business. Safer ground than getting personal again with Steve. "Still, there must be something in court records. That property must have sold after Bride died. He must have had some kind of will. Or maybe probate took care of it."

"I'm also waiting for info from a title company. I don't know how far back they have to search but it's gotta be long enough to please a bank."

She nodded, grooving on the hot soup. It was so rich and creamy, she had a feeling most of her chicken would come home with her.

"What are you going to the Castelle place for?" she asked.

"I want to explore the basement, see if noises could be rising from there up Vivian's wall. Then, tomorrow, the attic. Your help would be great."

"How so?"

"Somebody to listen in Viv's room."

Candy shook her head a little. "What about the parents?"

"I want someone totally objective in there. Not someone who's seen the dog react or heard some sounds herself."

Made sense. "You could solve this entire problem before your crew arrives."

"I hope. It'd be better for the family."

Again her approval of him rose another notch. Family before show. He wasn't kidding. "What happens if you can't do this program?"

He shrugged a shoulder and reached for his plate of chicken. "We'll do another. We're filming well in advance of air dates, so there's always something to plug in."

That made sense. "Do you always do these investigations by yourself, beforehand?"

"Mostly, except for a researcher off-site. I don't mind. I trust myself. If we find useful material, I can run through it as if it's the first time and it can be edited into a good story. Research *always* comes first. Period."

He'd told her that, but now she was beginning to believe him. A triumph for him, she supposed. Hostile deputy comes around.

STEVE WAS ACTUALLY looking forward to this part of his job. He had meters to take into the basement with him and find out if there were any anomalous readings down there. A high EMF could cause hallucinations in some people. Sometimes recorders picked up voices without an obvious source. Motion detectors could tell if something moved. Oh, yeah, lots of tech that he always worked in somehow, to reassure clients, to keep viewers watching.

The thing he was proudest of, though, was the lack of scam in what he did. Unless his producers called in a psychic. Those were the times he questioned what they were up to.

The Castelles greeted them warmly and Viv was excited to play a game of cards. He glanced at the parents and Candy.

"GO AHEAD," ALL OF them said, then the Castelles took Candy to their kitchen and offered her a drink.

"Water will be fine for me," Candy answered. She pulled her jacket off and slung it over the back of a chair. Annabelle gave her a tall glass of water.

"See?" said Todd, pointing to Candy's jacket hanging on the chair. "She's warm enough."

"Everyone's different," Annabelle replied. She was wearing a heavy fleece sweatshirt and pants, and another sweater was hanging over her shoulders. "Steve said he wants to check out the basement today and the attic tomorrow."

Todd sounded slightly irritated. "I already did that."

Annabelle frowned. "Yeah, but he's the expert, as you keep reminding me." She turned her attention to Candy. "Are you going to help?"

"Apparently. I get to stand in Vivian's room and listen to the sounds he makes."

"I did that," said Annabelle. "But it wasn't good enough. I only heard the sound that one time and Vivian wouldn't come in to listen."

Candy considered that problem. "Well, Viv's hearing voices, right? Maybe I'll hear something like that. Plus, he has all kinds of instruments he said he'll use."

Both parents relaxed a bit upon hearing that. More instruments meant more security, she guessed.

"I hope Viv can tell him some more," Todd said. "She's the only real witness."

Annabelle looked down, and for the first time Candy saw her shed a few tears. "We've *got* to help her."

"If this doesn't work, we're moving out," Todd announced firmly.

"But how? We sank everything into this house. Where would we go?"

"Anywhere else. I'll figure out something, I swear."

From the determination on his face, Candy believed he would. Good dad. Throw away everything they'd worked for so their daughter could have a better life and a dog. Just toss it on the trash heap to try again against all odds.

Steve returned with a grinning Vivian. "She beat me again. The odds favor her. We're going to have to try something a little harder soon. What do you think, Viv?"

"Oh, yes," said the little girl, sliding onto one of the chairs. "Can I have some chocolate?"

"Hot variety I hope?" Annabelle answered.

"Mmm. That's best."

"It certainly is for the amount of milk it gets into you."

Viv wrinkled her nose. "I don't like milk."

"Clearly," her mother answered drily.

Candy leaned toward her. "I don't like milk either," she confided. "Especially warm milk. So I drink a lot of cocoa."

"Me, too." Viv grinned. "And cheese. I love cheese."

"Now *that's* good," Candy agreed. "My favorites are Swiss cheese and white cheddar."

Viv pondered that. "I like lots of cheeses. Except American."

Annabelle laughed. "Too sweet for my taste."

Viv screwed up her face. "Some kids like it a lot. Just not me." Then she looked at Steve. "You're going to make the bad man go away?"

"I sure plan to try."

"That's good." She turned to her parents. "Can I take Buddy out to play?"

"Just bundle up," her mother answered. "We wouldn't want anything to happen to that cute nose."

Viv turned to look at Candy and Steve. "Can my nose really fall off?"

Steve laughed. "Only if it gets too cold. So listen to your mother."

Viv seemed okay with that, and Buddy was already getting excited, as if he understood what was coming. Even better, neither of the Castelles appeared troubled by Viv turning to someone else, in effect questioning them.

"Smart dog," Candy remarked.

"Almost as smart as Viv," Steve replied. "Ready to get started as soon as Viv's outside?"

"Absolutely." Although she had no idea of what she might hear, or how she had become involved in his experiment. Oh, well. After last night, she owed him this at least.

But it was interesting to watch him attack this problem alone. None of the showiness she would have expected. As if he wanted to solve all this as fast as he could for Viv's sake.

Oh, hell, she'd never wanted to like him. This wasn't going according to plan. But whatever did? She'd certainly learned in the Army that plans were great, but never worked as well as they sounded. Never. Too many unpredictable things in the mix.

After Viv and Buddy disappeared out the back door, Steve stationed Candy near the wall where Buddy had alerted. Seemed like a good starting place, even to Candy. Then he handed her a radio.

"Another one?" she joked.

"Just for you and me. Tell me anything you hear. I'm not going to let you know what I'm doing."

She nodded and watched him leave the room. Maybe this was the wrong time of day to do this. She'd ask him later since Viv seemed to be hearing the voices at night.

She waited patiently as she heard him speak from the kitchen. Probably getting information about the basement.

Nope, not what she'd been expecting to do at all.

Then she thought of Viv. That little girl shouldn't have to live with terror. No way.

DOWN BELOW, Steve wended his way among boxes and furniture that looked at if it might have been in the house when they bought it. Maybe they thought they could use some of it. The odor down there was musty, exactly like most basements.

When he reached the back of the basement, near Viv's room, he immediately noticed that in order to be right under the child's room, the basement needed to extend farther. He'd ask about that when he was done.

In the meantime, he had other things to take care of. He imagined this was the area Todd had checked out. There didn't seem to be any other place to go.

He set up his EMF detectors around the basement. If electromagnetic fields were involved, he wanted to know where they were strongest. Plus, not everyone had a problem with them. At least not the kind that would cause hallucinations of any sort.

But Viv might be sensitive to them, and this was an old house. It might have hidden wiring problems.

He positioned motion detectors as well, although they'd be little use while he was down here. But later he'd ask the parents to listen for their going off. Or maybe he could just get back here to pay attention himself. He still really needed some local lore and a way to fact-check it. If Candy was willing, she'd probably be an invaluable resource.

He found a sawed-off two-by-four and used it to bang on a pipe. He couldn't imagine that sounding like anything other than it was. Then he checked the heating ducts to see if any part was even a tiny bit loose.

He called Candy on the radio. "Anything?"

"Banging pipes," she answered drily.

He grinned into the radio although she couldn't see it. "About what I expected. A bit longer, if you don't mind."

"We aim to please."

Ouch, he thought. She really wasn't happy about this. Not that he could blame her. A deputy turned into an unwilling ghost hunter? Ha. Yeah, she'd love that.

He walked around checking the EMF meters. Only one place showed an elevated reading, right by the breaker box. Not unusual, and not high enough to cause concern for Viv.

Damn, he needed to find a way to help that child. A good reason that would help her and calm her parents. He hadn't the least doubt that no matter their outward calm around Viv, she could still sense their response to what she was experiencing.

Kids were gifted that way, with innate sensitivity to stress around them. Hard to fool. He wished parents would be more truthful with their children when they were upset.

Anyway, none of his business. He had a more immediate concern, a little girl he needed to help. And the potential for some outside threat against the family. That still concerned him, that the Castelles might have fled some threat at their previous home. Or that something unpleasant was going on in their marriage and a child was being used as a weapon.

There was one thing he could say about his current occupation. As a detective, he too often arrived in the wake of a tragedy that had broken lives. In this job, he could arrive beforehand and try to help. Depending. Always depending on what was going on.

His recorder had been running all the time, collecting any unheard or unnoticed sounds in this basement. Now it would collect him, too. Ugh.

Then he cleared his throat and began talking to himself in an ordinary conversational voice. Man, he hated this. He always felt like a fool talking aloud with no one there. But he'd known people who did it all the time.

Like his great-grandmother. He'd asked her when he was a child why she did that. Her answer was both excellent and a lesson he'd remembered his whole life:

"Sonny, when I talk to myself I keep my secrets."

An interesting way to think about it, but it wasn't feeling like that right then. Nope, it just felt silly.

After about ten minutes, he quit, glad to be done with it. Then he radioed Candy. "Anything?"

"Not a thing," she answered. "What was I supposed to hear?"

"Nothing. I'm going to keep on for a few more minutes."

"Roger that."

He cleared his throat. He wasn't the world's best singer by any means, but he chose a favorite hymn that didn't require him to be a Pavarotti, or even a record-

ing artist. It was also one that he knew the words to:
"Amazing Grace."

Amazing grace! How sweet the sound,
That saved a wretch like me!
I once was lost, but now am found,
Was blind, but now I see.

HE FELL SILENT, listening to the quiet of the basement,
then keyed the radio. "Anything?" he asked.

Candy replied. "I thought maybe I heard some very
faint singing. Did I?"

Well, a step forward. "Be glad you didn't have to
listen full volume. It's probably the only song I could
sing without sounding like a dying animal. I'm on my
way up."

He retrieved his recorder, turning it off, and headed
upstairs, where he found Candy waiting in the bedroom. "So singing was it? Believe me, the conversation I had with myself wasn't a comedy routine. I just
felt stupid. You ever do that?"

She smiled widely. "Not too often. And I feel silly
when I do. But no, I didn't hear anyone talking. Just a
very, very faint singing."

"Okay, then. More equipment in an empty basement tonight."

"Like what?"

"Cameras. A couple of digital recorders. I think I'll
put them in Viv's room, as well."

"Sounds like a plan."

He gave her credit for not acting as if he'd lost his
mind. She'd made it clear enough what she thought of
this shtick.

They went out to talk to Annabelle and Todd. Viv

was in another room with Buddy, whose tail thumped like a loud metronome.

"I'm going to bring back some equipment tonight to set up in the basement and in Viv's room. Just leave it all running and stay out of the basement."

Both Castelles sounded okay with that. In fact they sounded relieved that something was actually being done about their problem.

OUTSIDE, CANDY LOOKED at Steve. "You didn't mention that I heard you singing."

"On purpose. That's nothing to go on yet. All they'll know is that I made some noise. That won't help Viv's problem."

Candy frowned. "You're right."

"Besides, it was me down there. I'm sure they've gone down there when Viv heard the voices. I doubt they found anyone, or the problem would have been over before I got here."

He had a good point. That was when her stomach made an embarrassingly loud growl.

Steve laughed. "You need to eat."

"It sounds that way. I'm going to the market for a sub. They make decent ones."

"And here I thought I was becoming a fixture at Maude's."

She shook her head. "If that's what you want to do, go ahead. Maybe someone will talk to you seriously if I'm not there."

He paused. "What time do we go to Tate's?"

"He said eight."

"Okay. Where do we meet?"

"My place, seven thirty."

"You're on. And thank you."

Candy drove away wondering if he'd found anything useful or not. Apparently not, considering how much equipment he was planning to set up.

But while it had been very faint, she'd heard him singing. Not half-bad.

And an interesting choice of song.

Chapter Ten

"So Ben Wittes isn't a suspect?" was the first question Steve asked when he entered Candy's house.

"We sure don't think so. But nobody's ruled out yet. If we can find someone else, of course." Candy caught herself. He was familiar with how this worked. Sometimes she forgot his background. Well, he knew the procedure better than she did.

He just nodded, seeming unoffended by the rookie explaining the obvious to the pro.

"Tell me about the former sheriff," he asked as they drove toward Nate's house.

"His name is Nathan Tate, known everywhere as Nate. Regardless, I understand he came from the wrong side of the tracks, as they say. Went to Vietnam at eighteen, served in the Green Berets."

"That's impressive."

"It is," she agreed. "Anyway, a few years after he came back from the war, after serving with the sheriff's department, he was elected sheriff and remained in the job until he retired. After that his forensics expert succeeded him. Gage Dalton."

She snorted, feeling a sudden amusement.

"What?" he asked.

"Gage doesn't seem like a man people around here once called *hell's own archangel*."

"Seriously?" He twisted on his seat. "I've been wondering about his story since I met him."

"A helluva story. He was DEA. Undercover. His cover was blown. He was targeted with a car bomb that killed his wife and kids and he was badly burned. Someone told me he screamed so much after learning they were gone that he permanently ruined his voice."

"My God!" Steve fell silent.

"Yeah. The tragedy is damn near incomprehensible." Except she'd seen variants of it before, in war. War was an atrocity-making situation, something that was hard to live with afterward.

She shoved those thoughts back. Not now. She was as interested as Steve in what Nate Tate might know about the history of the Castelle house. God knew he'd been here long enough to have heard *something*.

But then so had Miss Emma. Surprising, the silence surrounding the Castelle house. Candy had begun to think everyone around here knew nearly everything there was to know about this area.

"Heard anything from the recorder's?" she asked as they pulled up before the Tate house.

"Not yet. Maybe another couple of days. I suspect someone is spending a whole lot of time sneezing from dust."

She laughed. He could be funny at times.

Together they walked to the door and were soon greeted by the former sheriff himself. He wore his years exceptionally well, only a dusting of gray in his dark hair, with the lines of a face marked by years of wind and sun. His voice was deep, a bit gravelly, and even at his advanced age he still managed to be an imposing figure.

He invited them in, saying, "Let's go to the family room. Marge is out, but I like that room even if it's big for one person. This house rambles every which way, which is why you'll notice we're walking past bedrooms, offices and so on. It's practically a warren. We had six daughters and were constantly expanding. Anyway, I like it because of the memories. No kids hanging around with their friends anymore, and we rattle around in here like dried peas. We're thinking about selling."

Interesting view of the man, Steve thought. Six daughters? It must have been overwhelming at times. But he also liked a guy who'd choose a room because of the memories it contained.

The family room was large and warmly decorated. There were even some colorful beanbag chairs left over from an earlier time.

"Sit wherever you like," Nate said with a wave of his hand, then settled into a Boston rocker.

There were two sofas and an assortment of upholstered chairs. Candy picked a blue one, and Steve a green one. When she was seated, she pulled out her small notebook and a pen to write information down if need be.

Nate spoke. "I hear you're wanting to pick my memory. It's a long one, all right."

Steve leaned forward, resting his elbows on his knees and clasping his hands. "I want to do exactly that. Are you aware of the house the Castelle family moved into?"

Nate rocked slowly. "I know the house. Saw a young

family moved in. It'll do that place and this town some good. Need more young folks like Candy here."

Steve smiled and Candy felt her cheeks color a little. That was a sideways compliment, she thought. It touched her.

"Anyway," Steve continued, "it's like a cone of silence has dropped over that house. I'm having a devil of a time trying to learn its history. Who owned it before, are there any stories about it?"

"Now that's a place." Nate nodded as he continued to rock. "Became quite something when I was in high school, just before I shipped out. Old man lived there. His name will come back in a moment, but it's been decades since I really thought about it."

Candy's interest quickened. It was amazing how she was getting drawn into this story, her curiosity growing more with each day. That was a good description from Steve: a cone of silence. This in a town where it seemed that if you wanted to know what you were doing, you just had to ask a neighbor.

Nate spoke. "Let me go back to the beginning, as much of it as I know. During my misspent teen years, it was occupied by a man who lived alone. A hermit, in the truest sense. People hardly saw him. He chased away kids who turned up to have a good time. Antisocial, but some of that was understandable, mainly because he'd lost his wife and no one knew where she went."

Nate shook his head a bit. "Sad how people can seize on something like that. The guy just wanted to be left alone. Instead, some folks created stories that he'd killed his wife and she was haunting the property. I heard it became a thing for youngsters to go out there at night on ghost hunts. The old guy chased them off, sometimes with a shotgun."

Nate suddenly leaned forward, his gaze becoming intense. "I was young and foolish. Everyone that age is. But I wasn't foolish enough to buy that crap or think those thrill-seekers had any right to bother a grieving man."

Steve spoke. "I couldn't agree more."

Nate's gaze went from intent to piercing. "Isn't that what you're doing over there? Thrill-seeking for millions who want to get scared in the security of their own homes?"

Man, Candy thought. *Full-frontal attack.* And clearly Tate was still as plugged into this county as he'd always been. She'd heard there wasn't a person or a secret that Nate didn't know. He was certainly up to date.

"What I'm here for," Steve said firmly, "is to help a seven-year-old girl who's scared to be in her own bedroom. She thinks a man is talking to her, one she can't see. And in case you're curious, her parents have even taken her to a child psychologist. Anyway, helping that child is my priority, and if I can get it done before we start filming and unless that family still wants to do the show, we won't. Plain and simple."

Tate's eyes narrowed, as he digested what Steve said.

"I also have a reputation to preserve," Steve continued. "I'm hunting for reasonable, logical explanations. I am not hunting for a ghost, and frankly I haven't met one yet."

For the first time since their arrival, Nate smiled faintly. He nodded, then rocked for a few minutes.

"All right, then," he said presently. "Let's talk about

the house. The stories kept growing while I was overseas. It wasn't enough that the wife had disappeared. Nope. Then it was claimed the old man had killed some teens who had trespassed. For some reason, by the time I got back, the tales had stopped in their tracks. I heard some talk about it all becoming campfire stories after that. Maybe the talk of murders shut it down."

"That's interesting," Steve remarked. "Were there murders?"

"I don't know. Seems like that might have turned this entire county upside down, and the old man would have died of something other than natural causes. I never looked into it. Wasn't part of my job, not an open case, and I wasn't especially tuned in to what teens were telling themselves sitting around a fire. I'd been away for eight years, didn't come back but once for a lot of reasons. Dead history by then."

Steve looked at Candy. "Would you be willing to look into this? Murders? Did the wife just run away?"

Candy nodded. She felt a strong need to know if this county had swallowed murders quietly and if so why. As for the wife? If there was an explanation, she'd find it, not that it would change much of anything. What people said to each other couldn't be silenced by an official explanation. But then, people liked a good conspiracy theory. If anyone years ago had claimed to have found the wife in Denver or New York, some would have insisted it was a cover-up. "I'll check it all out."

"Good," said Nate, leaning back again. "If this is going on, then it's not dead history after all. At best it could help a kid. At worst it could fire up all the legends again. As if folks don't already have enough to talk about." He cocked his head a bit to one side. "Well, around here I guess there's never enough for people to talk about."

Steve flashed a smile. "I've already begun to notice that."

"As for since then, there've been a couple of absentee owners. Probably thinking the land would be a good investment, which it might be if ever this town got back on its feet economically. There's hardly a building boom. At least they kept the place from going to ruin. Put some people to work with their money fixing things up, then eventually it went back on the market. This new family is the first to actually move in."

"Now that's definitely interesting," Steve said.

"I always thought so when I thought about it at all. Empty houses don't create a lot of police work unless they're vandalized."

Steve nodded. "No kids breaking in?"

Nate snorted. "Probably too afraid of a ghost with a shotgun. Yeah, I imagine old man Bride became part of the lore, too. Just too good to pass up."

Nate drummed his fingers briefly on the arm of his chair, then said, "I hear you were a cop once, Steve."

"Yes, sir. Detective after six years on the street."

"Good job. Anything else?"

"If I think of questions, can I call you?"

Nate smiled. "Hell yeah. I got plenty of time to reminisce these days. Candy has my number, obviously."

Candy laughed. "I've plagued you enough."

"Didn't mind at all. I hear there were two kids killed up near the old mining camp. Anything yet?"

Candy shook her head. "Early days."

"It would be. Sometimes I miss the harness. I generally behave myself and just bug Gage. He takes it well."

Candy grinned. "He'd have to. He's just the new sheriff after all."

It was Nate's turn to laugh. "Poor man. Well, hell, I get to be the old sheriff, so maybe *I* should complain."

Steve spoke. "You said the hermit's name was Bride. I've heard the last name before, just recently."

"It did come back to me, didn't it? Yeah. Samuel Bride. Wife was Ivy."

Candy jotted it down.

Nate turned back to Steve. "Let me know if I can do anything else."

Steve was nothing if not bold. "There is one thing. If we get to taping this show, would you mind doing an interview about the lore surrounding the house?"

"Why not? It's time that man's memory got laid to rest. And Candy?"

"Yes, sir?"

"You find out anything about what happened to that woman, let me know, too?"

She was happy to agree. "It would be nice to figure this one out."

OUTSIDE AGAIN, CANDY paused to look up into the night sky. "So many stars here. Like Afghanistan."

"Less city lighting," Steve answered, but he watched her closely. A beautiful woman who didn't deserve the memories she carried, and he hoped like hell that staring up at the stars didn't bring any of them rushing back.

She'd probably hate to realize that he was feeling protective toward her. A ridiculous thing to feel when she was evidently a very strong woman, and when there wasn't a damn thing he could do about her memories. He just hoped she made some new, good ones.

But the murders had really shaken her. He wondered how hard she was hanging on to her thoughts.

Then she lowered her face, smiled and started walking toward the car. "That was fascinating."

"I thought so. It sounds like most of the scary stuff was made up."

"That's what I thought, but I'll look into it."

"But, of course, none of this tells me why a little girl is hearing voices in her bedroom. And none of it tells me if this is threat to her or that family."

Candy paused with her hand on the car door. "You mean as in physical threat?"

Steve's insides tightened. He didn't like to think of these possibilities. Unfortunately... "I came here expecting to find something relatively innocuous to help the Castelles out. But if a real person is doing all this, then I need to wonder why. Anything I think of doesn't look good."

Candy looked poleaxed, but there was no point in pretending. He'd been ignoring the feeling that had been growing slowly in him since yesterday. A psychic, a spirit and two murders?

He'd been a cop too long to be a great believer in coincidence.

She looked at him over the top of the car. "But why? Who? My God, Steve, they just moved here."

"That doesn't necessarily mean a thing." He motioned her to get into the car, then slid in himself. With the doors closed, he felt more comfortable talking to her.

"It's like this," he said. "Any time I go into one of these cases, I'm looking for causes other than the paranormal. While it doesn't come out on TV, the fact is there are a lot of possibilities that are ugly. Lots. I'm a cop, I've seen too much to think that what looks like cotton candy on the outside doesn't have a cyanide pill at the center."

She stiffened at the wheel, and even in the dim light he saw her hands tighten around the steering wheel. "Damn," she breathed.

"Yeah, it's a terrible world. My thoughts run along ugly paths. But take the Castelles' situation. They moved to the middle of nowhere. Why? For a backyard? Or to leave something in the past? What if their relationship is rotten at the core? Or if one of them is? What if one of them is *using* Viv in some way."

He turned his head a little and saw her staring straight at him in the dark.

"That's just…" She seemed unable to find the words.

"I know. But you've been around, Candy. You know how horrible people can be. That child needs help. That means I look at every possibility, no matter how unthinkable it would be to most people. That's the part of this job that I don't talk about on screen or even in blurbs. It doesn't have to be ghosts. It doesn't have to be creaky plumbing or bad wiring. It can also be bad people. I don't skip looking into that."

He and Candy parted ways at her house. "I have to get my equipment out to the Castelle place for the night investigation. See you in the morning? I'll stop by with coffee."

"Sure."

He was aware of her eyes on him as he went to get into his rental.

And after listening to Nate Tate, the tension in him was growing stronger.

Maybe he'd been a cop too long. Or maybe he was right. If he was, he *had* to find out what was going on as quickly as possible.

BEN WITTES WISHED he could stuff cotton into his brain to shut the spirits up. They'd become excited about something and were yammering like a classroom full of kindergarteners.

Damn it. Imagine that the one strong voice in his head had been right about coming murders. The thought chilled him to the bone.

But the voice had been wrong about one thing. The murders weren't coming, they had already happened.

He clung to that, wanting no more even slightly accurate information about such things.

He wanted to give voice to the spirits lingering around that house, but not this kind of voice.

Although he didn't have much choice, like today.

Possession. The word floated into his head once more. What if Samuel Bride was trying to say something? What if this spirit had taken over someone else?

And if it were Samuel Bride, how could he have had anything to do with yesterday's murders?

But that one voice seemed to be slowly taking over, driving him to make that awful introduction of himself to the Hawks guy.

Closing his eyes, he began to pray for salvation.

Chapter Eleven

Steve set up his equipment that night, climbing into the attic to add more. The attic was huge, big enough to finish for a couple of bedrooms, but the only wiring visible led to lights at the head of the stairs and in the middle.

It was possible, however, that sounds might be transmitting from the attic down the wall to Vivian's bedroom. If he didn't pick up anything tonight, he'd bring the rest of his equipment up here for tomorrow night.

A good thing he had an unexpected tendency toward the technical, because one of the cameras wasn't working right, and he knew how to fix it.

In Viv's bedroom, he set up a wide-angle camera and a couple of voice recorders that would activate only if there was a sound. Best he could do unless he wanted to stay all night.

Not tonight. A scan of his earlier recordings had detected nothing but the heat turning on and the rattling of a duct that needed tightening. Not very useful since voices were the problem.

Downstairs again, he found the Castelles sitting in the kitchen over small snifters of brandy. A pleasant way to end the day. Vivian had apparently already gone to bed in her parents' room.

"How'd it go?" Todd asked.

"Pretty much blanketed. Hey, I needed to ask you a question."

"Sure, have a seat. Brandy?"

Steve smiled. "Don't get me started. I have to drive."

Annabelle laughed quietly. "Thus speaks the former cop."

But Todd took a different direction. "About your question?"

"Yeah. Brandy diverted me. So, about the basement."

Both Castelles leaned forward eagerly.

"I didn't catch anything today. That doesn't mean it isn't there, so after I do this part, I may need to get more intensive. More equipment maybe or spending the night in Viv's room. We'll see. But the basement."

"Yes?" Todd prompted.

"It's not big enough. As near as I can tell, it doesn't run under Vivian's room."

Annabelle spoke. "It doesn't. We noticed that, too, but the real estate agent explained it."

"Yeah," said Todd, jumping in. "He said that Viv's room was an add-on, and no basement was ever dug as far as he knew."

"Sitting on blocks." Annabelle nodded. "A good, firm base, the building inspector said, one that completely surrounds the room. No crawl space. We didn't worry about it after that."

A room with no basement. Steve wondered if he needed to deal with that somehow. If he could, short of tearing it all down. Hell. But if there was no basement, then how much could be down there? Some field mice? A rat or two? None of them would make voices.

He rose. "I'll leave you to your evening, then." On the way to the door, he paused. "Still hearing from old friends?" he asked casually.

"All the time," Todd answered. "Good friends are never left behind."

"Good." He smiled as he exited the house, thinking that problems never got left behind either. He hoped Dena, his researcher, would get back to him very soon. She was a wizard at getting public records that painted a background of his clients.

He drove past Candy's house on his way to the motel. Lights glowed from the windows, and he had the strongest urge to stop in. He wanted to learn more about her, beyond her Army career. Did she have family? If so, where? Were they close? What was the rest of her background?

This time it wasn't a cop's curiosity, it was a man's. Oh, trouble there, he warned himself. He didn't want to get attached to this place, especially a woman in this town. He traveled too much. His home was in Southern California and mostly he liked it. He doubted Candy would consider moving down there.

Hell.

He pulled up in front of her house and decided to knock even though it was nearing midnight. She could always tell him to drop dead. Besides, after last night, he was a little worried about her. What if her memories were still plaguing her?

Freaking excuse, that's what it was. Too bad. He got out of the car anyway, walked up to her door and knocked.

After a minute, she answered, looking surprised. "Steve!"

"Hey," he said with a pleasant smile. "I was thinking of going to Maude's before she closes to get a piece of pie. If you're interested, I'll bring you one."

Because he knew a cop never really felt off duty in a public place.

A slow smile grew on her face. "Apple, please, with a latte if you don't mind."

"I just hope she has some peach pie or cobbler left."

Well, that had gone well, he thought as he drove to Maude's. Now he only had to hope that the dragon would share some of the gold with him. Not that he really doubted it, but it was a fun thought about such a grumpy woman. He was beginning to wonder how she'd ever managed to have a kid.

Instead, Maude proved to be in a closing-shop mood.

"I got a piece of apple, and a couple of pieces of peach cobbler. You can have them just to clear out my display. No charge."

He beamed at her. "Very generous of you."

"Just don't like to throw away good food. I'll be baking fresh at four in the morning."

He watched her box the goodies. "How do you keep up this pace?"

She frowned. "It's the way of being in this business. Anything else?"

"Two of your biggest lattes, if it's not too late."

"For some folks, it's never too late to have coffee."

That was true. As a cop, he'd learned to depend on it for fuel.

Then he took a plunge, expecting to be rebuffed.

"You hear anything about the incident on the mountain, I guess it was?"

Maude handed him the first latte, already capped. "Two murders, I'm hearing. Folks are getting uneasy. Maybe even a little afraid. They're also wondering why this happened right after you came to town."

Steve's stomach lurched. "They think I'm a killer?"

"Right now, new faces don't help the uneasy. They're wanting it to be a stranger, not a neighbor."

"Ugh," he answered even though he could understand. "And Ben Wittes?"

Maude snorted, giving him the second coffee. "Crazy man. Most people just try to stay clear. Talking about spirits? I'm a religious woman, but I don't believe god loses souls, so what would they be doing hanging around to bother people?"

Good question, Steve thought. On the other hand, what if free will extended past death? It was a conundrum, if you thought about it. Occasionally he wondered.

But talk about garrulous. He wondered how he'd gotten so far into Maude's good graces. And he suspected he'd never know.

CANDY WAS KIND of glad Steve had stopped by. Her own ghosts were rattling the bars of their cage and threatening to escape. God, she needed to bury them for good, but she doubted she ever would.

Steve returned with two foam containers, and two coffees in one of those cardboard trays. "Grab a coffee before I drop it. These damn things barely support them."

She obliged, grabbing both of them. "Kitchen?"

"Best place to eat pie unless you want crumbs all over your living room."

He followed her.

"I want to vacuum as little as possible."

He laughed. "Every time I get back home, I hire a crew. I am definitely not the mopping or dusting type."

"I have to be. My mom always had a spotless house, aided by her kids. Then the Army took hold and taught me how to clean boot scuffs off a floor with a toothbrush."

"Seriously?"

She cocked an eye his way as she put the coffees on the table. "They had to keep us busy somehow when we didn't have other duties. But actually I think that was just another layer in teaching us who was boss, and to follow orders."

He could see that. But what a miserable job.

"White-glove inspections aren't just a myth. Try to survive one in bathroom facilities." She looked at him. "Plates and forks?"

"Please. Once in a while I need to pretend to be civilized."

That caused her to smile crookedly. She retrieved the plates and utensils, then sat facing him. He opened the containers and told her to help herself.

"That's a lot of pie and cobbler!"

"It is. Maude was cleaning out for the night and said she hated to throw away good food. No charge."

Candy lifted her eyebrows. "How'd you get on her good side?"

"Damned if I know." He watched Candy reach for the apple pie, then took a large square of peach cobbler for himself.

She indicated the pie. "That's two slices, I swear."

"So enjoy it." He ate a mouthful of cobbler, then said, "Maude told me something interesting."

"Yeah?"

"The town is uneasy about the murders. And they seem to be zeroing in on me. Stranger in town, arriving just before they happened."

"Oh, man." She paused with a piece of pie on her fork. "Another problem. I didn't expect that."

"Well, it makes sense under the circumstances. As Maude said, nobody wants to feel a neighbor could have done this. She also told me that Ben Wittes is crazy and people avoid him like the plague."

"I can believe that." She resumed eating. "It's not going to make your job easier if people are suspicious of you."

"I doubt it'll make it any harder. Trying to get information I can use in any way is like pulling teeth around here. Even public records. But you're going to look into the disappearance of Ivy Bride?"

"Absolutely. Nate piqued my curiosity."

They ate in quiet companionship, then Steve risked blowing the whole thing up. "Got any family?"

"Back in LA? Tons. A huge family."

"How are they doing?"

"Well, it seems."

But he'd noticed a tension coming over her and the remaining pie seemed to lose her interest. Maybe he should drop this right now. But he couldn't.

"You see them often?" he asked.

She shook her head.

"Family squabble?"

"Nothing like that." She dropped her fork onto her

plate. "You want the truth? The war changed me in ways I don't like. I don't want to go back and face a hundred family members who'll all be wondering what happened to me. Who might start asking well-meaning questions. I don't want them to see the new me. Then there's my brother."

He waited, but nothing more seemed forthcoming. Her eyes were beginning to take on that absent look again. Oh, God, what had he precipitated with his endless curiosity? It was one thing to push a witness or a perp, another to press a friend.

But then she found voice again. "My brother followed me into the Army. I think it was because of me. Back then I was all excited about the possibilities. Then he got killed in the 'Stan. I wouldn't be surprised if they blame me for that. And maybe they should."

His heart had squeezed so tight that he doubted he'd ever draw breath again. God, the weight this woman bore on her shoulders. It had to be crushing her a piece at a time.

He wished he could hug her, but he wasn't sure it would be welcomed. He didn't even dare offer the trite advice *maybe you should call them*. That was something she needed to decide on her own.

He felt useless except to say, "Maybe he was following in your father's footsteps. The way you did."

"Sorry," she said presently. "I shouldn't dump on you."

"I don't mind. Really."

She picked up her fork again and began to eat pie with determination. "Thanks for the pie and coffee. It's delicious."

Locking away the entire conversation. He understood that, too. But this woman was a box of sealed secrets, and short of a pry bar he didn't know how to get her to open up. It would probably require the kind of trust they didn't have yet.

"Thank Maude," he answered, hoping to lighten the moment for her. "She totally floored me."

Again a small smile, as if it were almost painful. "I hear she can be surprising at times. Never happened to me, though."

"Maybe she has a thing for handsome men."

That startled a short laugh out of her, and she began to look more relaxed. "So you've got an ego?"

"Of course. I just hide it well."

Her smile widened a tiny bit. Maybe that's all he could hope for just then. The murders had been really hard on her, and it might be taking some time to come back from them. Maybe she never would.

People with caring hearts and strong consciences often carried guilt like hers, even when it wasn't justified. It was awful, though, that she felt responsible for her brother's death.

He supposed a psychologist would remind her that her brother had a mind of his own, that she was depriving him of his own autonomy to think he'd joined the Army solely because of her. Or maybe a psychologist wouldn't say that. He wasn't one himself and wasn't going to dip his toes into those waters.

A few minutes later, Candy spoke again. "You're seriously considering that the Castelles, or one of them at least, might be behind this?"

"No stone unturned," he tried to say lightly. Maybe it was the cop in him, but he'd found that if a guy narrowed his focus too much on a presumed idea, then he could miss important things.

"Doesn't seem possible," she answered. "Not from what I saw anyway."

"Nope. But the public face is often different from the private face. You wouldn't believe some of the criminals I've locked up that everyone thinks is nice, pleasant, wouldn't hurt a fly. Some things just can't be believed, at least not safely."

She nodded, putting down her fork, the pie only partly eaten. "I can see that. It still doesn't seem possible."

"Maybe it isn't. But what matters here is one small child, not anyone else."

At last her tension seemed to be fleeing, her shoulders growing more relaxed, a half smile coming to her face. "Maybe you're right. The family seems too pat."

"Exactly. As if they emerged from a TV show from fifty or sixty years ago. It's always possible that they're exactly what they look like."

But nothing left to chance.

Then his cell phone rang. Courtesy made him ask, "Okay if I take this?"

"Please."

He'd never understand how some people thought it was okay to answer a phone even if they were in the middle of a conversation. When had phones taken precedence over everything else?

Well, his just had, he decided. Even though he'd asked, which most people didn't. As if everyone was supposed to understand that a phone call was more important than they were.

He didn't bother leaving the table. His latte was

there and, more important, he wasn't aware of any secrets that were likely to come across the phone. Candy was welcome to listen if she cared to.

It turned out to be his researcher. "Dena," he said cheerfully. "Got the dirt for me?"

"You bet," she answered. "You might want a pencil and some paper."

He paused. "That much?"

"Mostly basic details."

"Give me a minute." He lowered the phone and looked at Candy. "My researcher. You have any easy to access paper and pen?"

She rose and pulled the memo list off her refrigerator, and a pen out of a holder that was stuck there, as well.

"Thanks." He put the phone to his ear. "I'm ready, Dena."

He listened, scribbling down some high points. "You emailing that to me? Thanks a bunch."

"You owe me a scotch next time I see you."

Steve laughed. "You got it."

When he disconnected, he sat for a minute, thinking. Then he looked at Candy. "That perfect little family?"

She leaned forward. "Yes?"

"Todd's got a conviction for possession of drugs. They tried to nail him with trafficking."

Candy drew a sharp breath. "My God. You were right."

"Perfect on the outside, maybe not on the inside. How would you look at this?"

She hesitated visibly. "Nothing good springs to

mind," she said eventually. "But you're the experienced detective."

"Well, what I see is trouble. Todd could indeed have been trafficking. The amount at arrest may have been too small to convince a judge or a jury. I need the details. In the meantime, who knows who he was dealing with."

She nodded. "Damn, Steve. You were right. Who knows what they were running from?"

"Or who might be scaring their little girl. Todd doesn't sound like the pillar of decency anymore."

Chapter Twelve

Steve drove back to the motel, glad he'd decided not to babysit equipment tonight. Tomorrow would be soon enough.

He fought an internal battle with himself, however. His thoughts kept turning toward Candy, as if she were a lodestone and he was a piece of metal.

Damn, she was attractive. The urge to explore her every hill and hollow was beginning to preoccupy him entirely too much. The worst of it was, he didn't want to make her uneasy with some unwelcome advance. It had penetrated even his thick-skulled male brain that a lot of women hated it if they were made to feel like sex objects.

Not that he thought of Candy in only that way. Hell no. He liked plenty of the rest of her. She was smart and showed a restraint with him and his ghost hunting that he found admirable. So far she hadn't popped her cork and told him he was a conscienceless scam operator.

Nope. He even thought he might be winning her over to the possibility that he could be an honest man. Well, as honest as any person could be about themselves.

But the Castelles pulled him in a different direction. Todd had a drug conviction. He wanted to read his email from Dena to get all the details.

Because messing with drug gangs could get a whole lot more than messy. Because that marriage might not be as stable as it appeared on the outside. Because some unscrupulous sort thought he might torment Todd by tormenting his daughter.

Forget the psychic. There were bigger things afoot here than a self-deluded man who thought he was hearing voices.

He ran into the truck stop grill just long enough to get more coffee, then returned to his room, where he sat at the tiny table and opened his laptop.

He could read email on his phone, but he hated to unless the messages were short. *Old man*, he told himself. Not that he was that old, but he was way behind on this era of technology. Or at least in adopting it. People used to have face-to-face conversations, he thought. They'd sit down and talk to each other without reading their phones at the same time.

Then he almost laughed at himself. He wasn't old enough yet to turn into that guy screaming, "Get off my lawn!"

At least he hoped he wasn't.

Once again his mind tried to head back to Candy, but he yanked it away. Too many pitfalls, then add that to the likelihood that Candy wouldn't consider moving back to California—at least that's where he assumed she came from. She'd made her reasons clear for not wanting to go home again.

He hoped she'd get past that, but it was unlikely it would happen anytime soon. So what would he offer her?

A one-night stand, that's what.

Self-disgust filled him and he diverted back to the Castelles. As he read Dena's email, his concern about them grew.

Todd had been arrested, all right. For trafficking in drugs. The conviction for personal use had been granted by a judge who was evidently sympathetic to guys who were employed and had families. Or maybe because he was a handsome white guy.

An unbiased view of the criminal justice system said so. He'd seen enough cases to believe it, and much as he wanted to change that, he wasn't in the position. Charging was in the hands of the prosecutors. Convictions were in the hands of judges and juries, neither of which were totally impartial.

He sighed and continued reading. Todd had been sentenced to drug rehab, followed by community service for another year. He'd completed it all.

But that didn't mean it hadn't created stresses in that marriage. Maybe the family had moved out here to sever Todd's relationships with the wrong sort of people.

Or maybe they'd moved out here to get him away from drugs. Not a bad idea if it worked.

Or maybe they'd moved out here because he owed money to the wrong people.

The last one was the idea that concerned him most. There were some people on this planet whom you *never* wanted to owe money. People who weren't above killing you.

People who weren't above threatening you by showing how defenseless your kid really was.

Annabelle had mentioned they needed a bigger place to live that didn't exceed the constraints of their budget. He wondered if that was because they really didn't make a lot of money, or because they were trying to pay off someone.

Hell. This case had just grown complicated. It might not be about calming that family. It might be about protecting that little girl from very real danger.

Time to put on his detective's hat again. Time to get into that mind-set. He could do that without sacrificing his paranormal investigation. That much he still had to do.

Although ghost hunting had just taken a huge back seat to reality.

In the morning, just as the sun had begun to find its way into Conard City, he got a phone call from his producer, Etta Miller.

No holds barred on either side.

"Etta, this whole thing got complicated by a criminal past. I don't know if that's involved in this, but we may not have a show."

She sighed. "Steve, Steve, Steve."

"You know I don't lie to audiences."

"Yeah. I know."

"It was our agreement for me to do this program, so live with it. There are things I will not expose."

"I get it. But you'd better get on the stick with that psychic. He could be useful if this turns out to be on the up-and-up. Introduce him to the family to see how it works out."

Double damn, he thought as he ended the call.

But another thought wormed into his mind. What if the Castelles had been in hiding? Now that they'd been discovered, they might have thought that putting themselves on a nationally broadcast TV show could offer protection. With their identities out there, maybe no one would dare touch them.

He'd seen too much of this stuff when he'd been in law enforcement. He'd thought he might never see it again.

So much for pipe dreams.

CANDY HAD FALLEN asleep the night before thinking about what Steve had learned about the Castelles. If that were true, then this county might get a national shakeup whether people wanted it or not. Drug rings? What if that was ongoing?

She was supposed to be preventing that kind of stuff. Ha! Fat chance on this one.

But she woke in the morning from a much more pleasant dream. About Steve having remained last night. About the two of them making love.

As her eyes opened, her body felt flushed but she also felt like warm honey from head to toe. Softened. Pliant.

Abruptly she threw back the covers and welcomed the chilly air in the bedroom. Crazy. Just crazy.

Any relationship with Steve would be abbreviated in a few short weeks. Hardly more than a one-night stand. She'd had that kind of relationship only once before in her life and had vowed never to repeat it. It hurt too much. It had somehow made her feel dirty, used.

Nope. Not gonna happen.

A hot shower helped a little, especially when she stepped out into the cold air onto the bathmat. All wet, she began to shiver. That'd quell any errant desires, she told herself.

Later, her stomach full of warm grits and cheese, she donned her uniform and headed to the office. Now she felt an itch to research the Castelles herself and she still had to search for Ivy Bride. She hoped she'd find the woman had moved to somewhere far away.

As for the Castelles, it felt counterintuitive to her for them to want to be on TV if they were running from anything at all, most especially bad people. Steve held a different opinion, and she wanted to hear more of his thoughts on that.

She'd seen a different look about him last night. Something darker, less lighthearted. Something so focused she wouldn't want to be the object of that gaze.

The detective, she supposed. That part she might not mind watching in action. She had plenty to learn.

But research was next on her agenda, and as she drove the official SUV that she'd parked at her house last night, she thought about which case should be her starting point.

Finding Ivy Bride struck her as important. Nate had been right. It was time to lay the man to rest, if she could.

The Castelles... Well, she didn't doubt that Steve would be hot on that case. He'd probably share with her, too, as he had last night.

This whole thing was getting a lot messier than she'd anticipated when she'd been assigned to liaise with a ghost hunter.

On the other hand, it had grown a lot more fascinating.

Once at the office, after greeting the others, she took a desk in the back of the wide-open duty area, away from conversations and distractions, and set to work.

Ivy Bride first. It proved easy enough to come up with the woman's maiden name, Haskell. She started the databases running, looking for obits for Ivy Bride, Ivy Haskell Bride and Ivy Haskell. Responses came slowly.

Well, yeah, she was searching a period sixty years ago. Many items hadn't been digitized, and when public records had made their way into databases, they were huge ones.

Taking advantage of the lost time, she went to Maude's to get coffee. If Velma scowled at her when she brought it back, Candy never noticed. It wouldn't surprise her if Velma was in on the joke and just never let anyone know. As she'd begun to discover, the woman could have a wicked sense of humor.

Velma was certainly too smart not to have noticed the collection of antacids against the wall behind the coffee mugs. Or maybe she was just stubborn.

In Velma's shoes, Candy would have tipped over the coffee urn and told everyone to get their own coffee. A big difference in temperament, which might be part of the reason Velma had kept her job for so long. Candy imagined that dealing with all these deputies, all the comms and all the crimes required a pretty calm personality.

When she returned to the desk, the computer search had started to turn up names. Sheesh, who would have thought there were so many women named Ivy Haskell. She was able to eliminate all of them by time frame. Born too late, couldn't possibly have lived to be one hundred and twenty. Not likely at any rate. Way too young to have been a married woman all those decades ago.

She worked at finding a way to narrow the search parameters even more by dates to reduce the number of results. She figured it out and put the computer to work again.

She also needed to hunt for name changes, she decided. Ivy Haskell Bride would have had to use her full name in order to change it by court order. Then there was always the possibility of a marriage. Just because Bride hadn't ever mentioned a divorce didn't mean there wasn't one. Plus, dissolution of marriage often gave a person a built-in way to change their name to anything they wanted.

So next, marriages and divorces. Then name changes. All public documents. But man, waiting for a computer to check public databases from all over the country was going to drive her nuts. She might as well go for a stroll, tap dance in the park or spend time at Maude's listening to the casual conversation as it wrapped around her.

Or she could just sit here with her coffee and practice the patience she had learned while standing post.

A while later, census reports started popping up. She found one for Ivy Haskell Bride, wife of Samuel Bride, all the way back at 1960, residence listed only as Wyoming. Ivy vanished before the 1970 census. Maybe the census had stopped providing public data on living individuals. If so, it must be causing headaches to genealogical researchers.

Well, that was another bracket. Name changes after 1960.

Death notices after 1960. She queried the Social Security database and found nothing. No death report filed there, probably because Ivy had never received Social Security.

The invisible, missing woman.

Several frustrated words ran though Candy's thoughts, but she knew she could dig even deeper if this didn't turn up more information. There were other databases available, mostly criminal and military. Neither one seemed likely for a farmwife of that era, but she couldn't skip them.

And, of course, she needed to check the sheriff's records to find out when the woman had been reported missing. If she even had.

The molehill was rapidly turning into a mountain.

It was also part of her job, whether for this Steve Hawks thing or some other reason. Being a cop wasn't always romantic or even interesting. Still, given how hard-won this position was, she wouldn't trade it in for anything.

STEVE HAD OTHER matters on his mind. Candy was dealing with Samuel and Ivy Bride. He needed more info on the Castelles before he went back out there.

Years as a detective had taught him that he could conceal his suspicions, and right now they were running high. He called Dena again.

"What, man?" she asked when she answered. "I gave you a bucketload."

"I know. But I wonder if you know any more."

"As if other stuff would be public record. I've got informants on the street, but if I target someone too closely, one of my people could get killed. I'll ask generally, but that may take a while. Basically, you're on your own."

He'd figured, but it never hurt to ask, especially when Dena's sources had proved fruitful in the past.

He thanked her and disconnected, then decided to wander over to the sheriff's before heading out to the Castelle place. He figured Candy might be hating him by now.

Being a cop often meant getting deep into the weeds of the world of records. Prior arrests, yeah, but general information on suspects and witnesses. Getting the word from the streets, which often came through other cops. Research until his eyes nearly fell out of his head. It sure wasn't a matter of walking around wearing a gun and badge like a big man.

Nope. It would have been even tougher if he hadn't had a team.

Candy had no team.

Get her a coffee, maybe suggest a quick lunch. Ask her if she could take a break and join him out at the Castelle house. She might jump at the opportunity by now.

A glance at his watch told him it was nearly noon. Yeah, she could use a break. Besides, he had an ulterior motive. He wanted to see her again.

The bug had bit him.

He found Candy at the back of the office, focused intently on a computer screen. She looked up when he said her name and her eyes refocused.

She spoke. "I suppose I don't have to tell you how much this sucks."

"Nope. Hence my invitation to lunch and maybe a trip to see the Castelles." He put a coffee beside her. "Or you can sit here torturing yourself for the next few hours. I'll come back and help you pick your eyes up off the floor."

That pulled a laugh from her. "Lunch it is." She took the cup and sipped the latte. "Fuel. Or maybe ambrosia."

"Well, then, let's go."

She rose, pulling on her jacket and picking up her cup. "Take me away."

His heart skipped, which it shouldn't have. "Glad to oblige."

Maude's didn't seem very busy for the time of day. They found a booth without any problem, and as they sat, Steve wondered if the murders had caused the emptiness. Were people so nervous they didn't want to come out to lunch? Or so nervous they wanted to keep an eye on their kids? Were kids even going to school?

"Have people gone into hiding since the murders?" he asked her.

"All I know is they're nervous as hell. I'm sure there have been cases of multiple murders here, if for no other reason than that sickos appear everywhere, but I'm not that far into the loop yet."

"If I were a parent, I'd be worried," he admitted.

Then Mavis appeared wanting their orders. Both of them were prompt. This didn't seem like a place you could dither for a while. He wouldn't be surprised if Mavis decided for them.

He went for clogging his arteries again, blaming it on the travel. Or excusing it. A succulent cheeseburger with fries and a side of salad. Candy had apparently given up fighting her appetite, too. No salad, which he was used to women ordering. No grilled chicken. Nope. Steak, corn bread and broccoli.

"Corn bread?" he asked.

She nodded. "Every so often. Love the stuff."

"It's pretty good," he agreed. "I never think of it."

Her answer was dry. "It's rarely on a menu. Besides, I don't like it dry, so I never make it at home."

She dug in happily, as did he. Then she asked, "Anything more that's interesting?"

"My researcher is going to gently sound out her street informants, but she doesn't want to draw attention to any of them."

"I have to admit I'm disappointed in Castelle," Candy admitted. "You'd never guess."

"And maybe that drug stuff is really all in the past. People do recover. But even so, I have to wonder what effect that might have had on their marriage."

"I can't imagine it was good. Maybe they're putting it back together. But the kid. Why would anyone want to torture that child?"

"To send a message. Let him know they've found him. Maybe he thinks this will draw him and Annabelle closer. I can think of a whole lot of motives. Anyway, my producer is hounding me. Work with the damn psychic."

He saw her lips twitch. "Have fun."

"Oh, yeah. Loads of it."

"You don't like psychics?"

Steve shrugged, certain he'd mentioned this before. Or maybe only inside his own head. "I've met a couple that I thought might be genuine. Can't really prove it, of course. Then there are those who walk around giving vague impressions that anyone could provide in the circumstances. Or those who just put on a show to make it look like they're doing something. I'm wondering which kind Ben Wittes is."

She cut another piece of steak. "But you allow the possibility?"

"I've learned not to dismiss anything without proof. I suppose it's possible that some are genuine."

Like ghosts. He just needed some really good proof. Hard proof. The kind he could take to court. How likely was that in this field?

After lunch, Candy ran over to the sheriff's office to check on the progress of her searches. When she came back, they both climbed into her official vehicle.

For once he was agreeable to that when visiting a client. It showed his involvement with the police in case something truly unsavory was going on.

"This search is going to take forever," she told him as she wheeled onto Main Street and drove toward the Castelle home. "I'm astonished how many Ivy Haskells there are. She did turn up in the 1960 census, though. Last time."

He gave a low whistle.

Candy shrugged. "At some point the Census Bureau stopped making names public as far as I can tell. It doesn't really mean much, except it gives me a search bracket. Name changes, divorces, police records, the whole deal."

"There must be a lot out there."

"As I'm discovering. What about you? Anything?"

"More questions at this point. Somebody's going to be facing legal trouble if they're harassing that little girl. Enough said."

Candy spoke slowly. "That drug conviction must have nearly destroyed their marriage."

"I thought of that. A lot here under that Donna Reed facade. Well, I'll find it out."

He always did. People's secrets had been his meat and potatoes as a detective, and that much hadn't changed.

"But why would they want to be on TV, considering the possibilities?"

"Cover," he said flatly. "They get national exposure, and if anything happens to them, it's not going to escape notice. Protection."

She drew a sharp breath. "I hadn't thought of that."

"Most people wouldn't. Under this friendly exterior lies a mind that is used to thinking the unthinkable. The not immediately obvious."

"I have a lot to learn."

"You're on the way," he said as they turned into the Castelles' driveway.

"This is going to be a learning experience."

"I hope not."

THE CASTELLES GREETED them warmly. Viv was out back with Buddy, and Steve and Candy were invited inside.

"Let me run around and check my equipment," Steve said. "Then I'll join you in that coffee."

"Help yourself," Todd answered.

Steve paused. "Anything last night?"

"Not that we were aware of. We were all hunkered down in our bedroom. As usual. Plus, we didn't want to bother your equipment, like you said."

Steve smiled. "Good job. If I hear footsteps on a tape, I want to know if it was you."

Annabelle laughed. "You may hear the thump-thump-thump of Buddy running around, though."

"I think that would be pretty distinctive." He disappeared in the general direction of the attic stairs.

Candy sat with them at their kitchen table. Like a lot of people, they seemed to prefer it to the more formal living room. It was hard now not to look at them with suspicion, so she turned the conversation in a safer direction.

"You ever consider finishing the attic?" she asked. "From the outside it looks huge."

"It *is* big," Annabelle answered.

"Nice," Todd agreed. "We could put a couple of spacious rooms up there. We've talked about a bigger office. Maybe an extra bedroom. And a bath, for those that don't want to run up and down stairs repeatedly."

Annabelle made a face at him. "I wouldn't be that someone, would I? Anyway, it would be expensive. We certainly couldn't do the wiring or the plumbing ourselves. But did you get up there, Candy?"

She shook her head. "No, not yet."

"When you do, take a look at the lath. It covers all the walls up to the peak of the roof, and someone stained it at one time. It's a work of art unto itself."

Todd laughed. "It's beautiful all right. Almost a shame to hide any of it."

"Excuses," Annabelle retorted. "Space. We came out here for space."

Candy couldn't help wondering if that had been the real reason.

"Anyway," Annabelle said, "our apartment in the city? Hardly any room. One bedroom, barely big enough for a bed. We had to turn the living room into our office and screen off an area for Vivian to sleep in. Then we had this kitchen that was almost too small to move around in."

"I've seen places like that," Candy said. Mostly in foreign countries where entire families lived in one-room shacks and cooked outside under lean-tos. Many of them probably would have thought the Castelles' apartment was a palace, but she could understand why they didn't.

Steve passed by on his way to the basement.

Annabelle spoke. "I don't know whether I hope he finds something."

"It could be worse," Todd answered.

"Since I heard those sounds, nothing would be worse. Trust me."

Todd slipped an arm around her and squeezed her from the side.

"It's true," she said. "I'd rather have a ghost than wonder if Viv and I are losing our minds."

"You're not," Todd said, giving her another squeeze. "I'm sure of that."

How could he be sure? Candy wondered. Because he knew something? Damn, she hated the suspicions Steve had awakened in her.

But it remained Todd couldn't know, even if it was highly unlikely that both wife and daughter were developing a mental illness at the same time. Or unless he suspected a cause for this that had nothing to do with mental health or ghosts.

Jeez, was this how Steve had to think?

She didn't envy his world at all. She'd lived with suspicion for too long in combat areas. Suspicions about every local she talked to. Sometimes suspicions about members of the local armies. That was some of the baggage she wanted to leave behind. To learn to be trusting again.

Steve returned about twenty minutes later. Conversation had revolved around exactly what Todd and Annabelle did for their living. Both of them appeared to become excited when they talked about it. Much of it was over Candy's head. 3-D graphics? Like in the movies? She didn't ask.

They also talked briefly about the conventions they had to attend to promote themselves and their work, but mostly to meet fans. The crowds. Candy was sure she would have shrunk in crowds that size.

Then Steve reappeared and joined them at the table, accepting a mug of coffee. "Nothing," he told two inquisitive faces. "But you were right about Buddy. He makes quite a ruckus when he runs."

"He's not at all light-footed," Annabelle said drily. "We always know where he is. So nothing?"

"Not yet. Two things. If you don't mind, I'd like to spend a night in Vivian's room. Listening. Maybe I'll hear something or get a brainstorm. Right now I could use one. The other thing is a psychic. My producer found one, and she's hot to try him out."

Annabelle leaned forward. "I'll try anything if it might help. I just need someone to find out if this is real and, if not, what might explain it. Bring a psychic. Bring the Army. Bring another building inspector." Her eyes teared up. "Anything except make my daughter live with this fear."

"Honey," Todd said. "We'll move."

"Not until we've tried everything," she said fiercely through her tears. "This is our dream. Every dime we have is right here. I want to fight for it."

Candy gave her props for that. A strong woman, determined to stand and fight. Fleeing sure as hell would have been easier.

Todd looked at Steve. "Nothing? Absolutely nothing?"

"Not yet," Steve answered. "One night doesn't mean a damned thing, though."

"Then you'll stay tonight?"

"I said I would. I generally like to do at least several nights by myself. When my crew gets here, I'll repeat it all, but you may want to take our invitation to find a decent motel so you don't have to live with the uproar. If you think spirits are noisy, try a film crew."

That at least made Todd grin. "I can almost imagine."

"Anyway," Steve continued. "Have you done any remodeling since you moved in?"

Annabelle started to shake her head, then stopped. "What do you mean by remodeling? Paint? Wallpaper? Or something bigger?"

"Moving walls? Making holes when you checked the electrical? Things like that. I keep hearing that renovations can disturb the spirits."

"Oh."

The couple exchanged looks.

"Well," Todd said. "I guess we have. I added some track lights in our office. And we had an electrician install more outlets that could handle the needs of our equipment."

Steve nodded. "Anything else?"

"We had some rewiring done, but that was in the barn. Place is a firetrap waiting for a spark. Useless until we can do more about it, but we still need some light in there. A fluorescent lantern wasn't cutting it."

"Great for camping, though," Steve joked. "Well, that sounds like enough to answer audience questions. Have to touch all bases, you know."

Annabelle lifted her head a bit. "You don't believe that renovations could cause this?"

Steve shrugged. "I'm in the business of not believing theories. I'm not sure when last someone actually talked to a ghost about what's bothering them."

Todd snorted. Even Annabelle managed a weak smile.

"That's the point, isn't it?" Steve asked, leaning forward. "If you want to confirm a preconceived idea about what's happening in this house, I was the wrong guy to choose."

Todd nodded. "That's why we came to you."

"I hope so. The unvarnished truth, if I can find it. That's my way."

Barely two minutes passed before they heard a knock at the front door. At the same time, Vivian burst in through the back door. The air around her and Buddy carried the outside cold.

"I'll get the door," Todd said, as Annabelle leaned forward to hug her daughter and start unzipping her outerwear.

"Chocolate, Mommy."

"You betcha!"

A happy little family, Candy thought. Hard to believe there was something dark behind them.

Then Todd walked in with a scruffy Ben Wittes, who looked as if he could use a shave.

"Ben Wittes," Todd said. "I believe he's expected."

Steve rose and shook the man's hand. As dirty as it looked, Candy didn't envy him.

"Good to see you again," Ben said.

Annabelle turned from the stove, where she was making Viv's hot chocolate, and murmured a greeting. She wasn't happy about this, although she claimed she was willing to try anything to help Vivian.

And Viv herself stared at the man, her eyes huge.

Candy couldn't blame her. Ben looked like something that had crawled from under a rock. When he smiled, the expression wasn't comforting.

Vivian slid off her chair and edged toward her mother.

"What do you want me to do?" Wittes asked Steve.

"Walk through the house with me," Steve said. "Give me your impressions."

Ben nodded. "I'm ready to start. The spirits have been ramping up since I began driving this way. Guess they have a lot to say."

Candy had trouble keeping a straight face. She waited to hear anything that might stand out from casual conversation. Something with meat on it.

"Do you mind?" Steve asked the Castelles.

"Go for it," Todd said. "No stone unturned."

Except, Candy thought, the one Ben Wittes had crawled out from under.

STEVE TURNED ON one of his recorders and began the walk-through. He wanted one thing, just one thing, that would justify making this man part of his show. If he couldn't get anything but a jumble of impressions anyone could have provided, he'd send the man packing and go to the mat with his producer, Etta Miller. He didn't usually have to fight her, but when he did, he stood his ground until she came around, or they could reach a satisfactory compromise.

But it was fair to give the man a shot at this, especially to placate Etta.

He just hoped someone would clean this guy up before filming. He looked downright disreputable.

He led Ben to the very back of the house, to the Castelles' bedroom. No activity had been reported in there, and it was a good test of Wittes.

"Go ahead," he told the guy, then waited with his recorder on. If the man provided anything useful, he wanted it on tape.

Ben closed his eyes and swayed a bit. Not terribly theatrical, which was good.

"The man is still here," he murmured slowly. "He hangs around all the time, doesn't want to leave."

Steve wanted to question him but waited. That was a pretty general statement, hardly worth paying attention to. Yet.

"He doesn't want to leave," Ben continued. "There are others here. A woman. She's angry."

Again, not much. Again, Steve waited.

Then Ben's eyes snapped open. "Over here," he said, and promptly walked along the hall to Vivian's bedroom.

"Here," he said firmly. "He likes this room. People in here might hear his voice."

That caught Steve's attention. Unless the Castelles had been telling others about this, it might be important. He'd have to ask after Wittes left.

Wittes closed his eyes again, and genuinely looked as if he were listening intently. "A dog senses him. The woman is here, too, still angry but she says nothing. Not that people might hear. She doesn't want to talk."

Ben turned and looked at him. "She was killed here."

All right, Steve felt a little prickle at the base of his neck but refused to give in to it. With the stories that had once floated around this town, the statement was meaningless.

"The woman likes a little girl. She wants to protect the child but doesn't know how."

Finally, Steve broke his silence. "Protect her from what?"

"The shouting man. The mean man."

Ben fell silent once more, appearing to listen intently. "He wants to shout louder because his words aren't being heard."

Not quite true, Steve thought. A voice was being heard, but the words weren't making sense. Or weren't audible enough to be understood.

Ben turned to look at Steve. "He says he didn't do it."

"Didn't do what?"

"Kill anyone."

"Most perps say they didn't do it."

Ben's lip curled upward. "Doesn't matter if you don't believe it. *He* believes it."

Point taken.

Wittes shrugged slightly. "Others are here, but I'm not sure they're attached to this house. They come to me from all over."

Sure. "How do you do this, Ben?"

"They talk to me. Because I can hear them. I'm done. I'm tired. Can I come back tomorrow?"

"I'll see."

As he watched Wittes leave, all Steve kept thinking was that the man had run out of material. What had he done to exhaust himself? Listen to nothing? Or try to act?

Steve made his way back to the kitchen. The first thing he saw was Vivian. She was pale, ignoring the cocoa in front of her.

"What's going on?" he asked her parents.

Annabelle answered. "I don't think she likes that guy. Not that I can blame her. I could smell him across the kitchen."

"Pretty ripe," Steve agreed. "You two ever tell anyone around here about what you're experiencing?"

Two heads shook negatively. "We even told Viv not to mention it at school."

Then Steve squatted beside Viv's chair. "Something wrong, sweetie?"

Her face started to clear and she reached for a spoon to pull out one of the small marshmallows. "Not invisible," she said.

Then she would say no more.

STEVE PROMISED THE Castelles he'd be back later to check his equipment and prepare to spend the night.

"I've got a sleeping bag I can offer," Todd said. "It's going to be chilly whichever room you're in."

But the ride back to town with Candy was silent until they approached the sheriff's office.

He was the first to speak. "Did you notice anything about Vivian while I was out of the room?"

"Only that she looked uneasy. Anyone would look uneasy around that man, especially a child. Nothing else, though. Once he was out of the room she sat at the table for her cocoa."

He nodded, thinking. Ben wouldn't appear to be the friendliest man, but he also didn't appear especially threatening. Still, for a child...

"What she said?" Candy asked. "About not invisible."

"That's bothering me," Steve admitted. "God knows what it meant."

"Did you learn anything useful?"

"Not really. Nothing he couldn't have pieced together from local lore. We'll see what he has to say tomorrow. I just hope I catch something tonight."

"Why?"

"Because I'll take anything that can convince those two parents that their daughter isn't nuts."

"I can agree with that. Well, I need to get back to my computer in the hopes that I can learn something about Ivy Bride. How often do people just vanish?"

"You'd be surprised. It's more common than most people think."

"Sometimes I've wished I could do that."

Candy's comment was nakedly revealing. It jerked his attention back to her, and he wished like hell he knew what to say or do. He offered lamely, "I'm glad you haven't."

"At the moment, so am I. More Wittes tomorrow?"

"It appears so. But I want to do something else."

"What's that."

"I'm bothered by the fact that there's nothing below Vivian's room. I want to take a close look at that foundation."

Oh, yes he did. And he wanted to call Etta and tell

her that Wittes wasn't going to look good on screen. Not at all.

If Etta wanted to try to clean him up, let her.

THEY PARTED WAYS at the office, and Candy went back to becoming an online researcher. She supposed she ought to be grateful that she didn't yet have to paw through dusty stacks of files.

To her pleasure, the database had spit out two matches: Ivy H. Bride had married James Flannery. And an Ivy Bride had changed her name to Ivy Cain. Candy made a note to add that to her search.

Hoping there was more, Candy resumed waiting. She didn't want to interrupt the search at this stage. Not yet. She could check on these names when no additional information popped up.

She hoped it would pop up soon, because she'd made up her mind to accompany Steve to the Castelles' house.

Because she wanted to judge for herself exactly what he was doing.

Suspicion kept gnawing at her. The psychic had increased it just by being called in. What if it hadn't been Steve's producer who had introduced Wittes? What if it had been Steve himself?

Then there were all the questions about the Castelles. The whole thing was getting awfully murky.

Chapter Thirteen

Steve was surprised, but not annoyed, when he found Candy parked out in front of his motel room in her official SUV.

Well, well, well, he thought as he joined her. Was she becoming interested? Or just answering her budding cop's instincts that something other than a ghost was going on?

"What did Wittes tell you?" she asked.

"Oh, some stuff about an angry man hanging around and a woman who was mad because she'd been killed."

Candy sighed. "Sounds awfully familiar."

"Yeah. But he gets another bite at the apple tomorrow. If he has no more to add that doesn't fit in with what Tate told us, he's out. As it is, my producer would have to run him through a car wash and a barbershop and buy him new clothes."

"Would she?"

Steve chucked quietly. "She'd have to. Think of audience reactions if he appears looking like he came off skid row." Then he paused. "Guess that's unfair to homeless people."

"It is," she agreed. "Many are vets, to begin with.

Then there's the fact you can only sink so low before you have no chance at a job anymore."

Steve knew that to be true. In his job he'd dealt with many homeless people, like one guy who worked six days a week as a dishwasher in a restaurant. Not enough money to get an apartment, but he wasn't at all what people thought of when they thought of the homeless. He'd heard too many stories like that.

"Are you planning to stay all night?" Steve asked her.

"Believe it."

He let it go. He was sure she had her reasons, but equally sure he wouldn't like some of them. Better not to know. Hell, she was probably suspicious of him again. She'd started there, so why wouldn't she finish there?

So much for his sense that she was coming to believe he wasn't running a con. Maybe Wittes had something to do with that. Well, he was wondering if Wittes was a con, too.

Some people, he reminded himself, just wanted the attention.

The Castelles welcomed them pleasantly enough and said the three of them were going to their bedroom for the night.

"No TV," Steve admonished them.

"We get it," Todd replied. "Can one of us at least read to Viv until she falls asleep?"

"Sure," said Steve. "Before it gets really dark, which is soon, I want to check out the foundation around her room. I've got some good light with me, so maybe we'll check out the barn, too."

"Be careful of your footing out there," Todd warned. "The floor is uneven and old."

Then the family disappeared into the back.

"The foundation?" Candy asked.

"Everything. It would make this easier if you'd shine a light from the far side as I go. I want to see if there are any openings at all."

"For rats or mice?" she asked humorously.

"For loose stones that might make a man-sized opening if they were moved."

He could see that she approved. Good. He was no fly-by-night who'd overlook something that obvious.

Then the barn, which could be a good hiding place since the Castelles rarely went out there, if they even had since they bought this land.

Barns. There were lots of spooky stories around them. It would please his fans to see him investigate a derelict outbuilding, not that that was his reason. Nope. He wasn't in the business of skipping over possibilities.

An hour later, the two of them sat on the cold-hardened ground, leaning back against the foundation.

"Something isn't right," Steve said.

"How so? We didn't find any light shining through anywhere."

"And that's what's wrong." He realized that he was sitting on a stone and lifted himself a bit to pull it away. "One stone. I always find it when sleeping in a tent."

She laughed quietly. "Me, too."

"Anyway, as to what's wrong. Does that foundation look like it's sagged anywhere?"

She thought for a minute. "Actually, no."

"Well, it should have, if it's sitting on bare earth. There must be a slab of some kind under that room."

"That tells us what?"

He stared toward the darkened hulk of the barn. "Maybe nothing. I couldn't see anywhere that it was open, and I sure didn't see anything in Viv's room that looked like even the smallest door. Besides, how would anyone get in there without becoming stuck for fear of discovery? I'll have to think about it."

"Yeah. I will, too."

"Anyway, tomorrow the barn." He'd changed his mind about doing it tonight. It was so dark he wasn't sure the few lights would be enough for the close search he wanted.

Even in the darkness he could sense her looking his way. "How could that possibly be involved?"

"I don't know. That's for me to find out. Come with?"

"Sure. I'm starting to enjoy this. What's next?"

That was good news, he thought. In a way it *was* like a treasure hunt.

"Let's go back inside. I'm planning to stay in Viv's room tonight to see if I can hear anything. I'm mostly convinced that some sound is traveling through her wall, either up or down. Or it could be a sound bouncing off the wall. I hope I get to hear it."

"And me?"

"I'd like you in the attic, close to that wall. Maybe you'll catch something." He paused. "I hope I can find something rational tonight, just to put that kid out of her misery."

"Let's go. It's getting cold out here."

"Yeah."

The house was warmer by far, however much he'd

been warned that it would be chilly. From the sounds, everyone was asleep now. Good.

"It's going to be cold up there," Steve said.

"Some of the house's heat will get up there. Anyway, I'm dressed for the outdoors."

"I hope you can get comfortable."

But there was nothing he could do about that. Maybe one of the lingering pieces of furniture would help with that.

First, he climbed to the attic to make sure all the equipment was working.

"Since we're listening for sounds, you can keep the lights on. Anyway, the mind tries to fill in the darkness."

"I'm familiar with that."

He supposed she was. Then he headed down to the basement and checked everything. If there were any noises down there, the recorders should catch it.

Then back to Viv's room. He debated whether to lie on the bed, then decided he could sit on the floor with his head against the wall.

Settled against the wall, he listened to a house as quiet as any could be. The heat kicking on, rattling the floor vents just a little. Wind against the windows.

And nothing that sounded remotely like a voice.

He settled in for a long, uncomfortable night.

AT ABOUT FOUR in the morning, he heard it. A faint voice, as if it came from far away. Too faint to make out words, but with the rhythms of speech.

Annoyed that he couldn't just start running upstairs and down, he hoped it wasn't too faint for the recorders to pick up. It shouldn't be.

Then the sound stopped. A few minutes later, Candy came down from the attic.

"Steve," she whispered. "Sorry for deserting my post, but I heard a faint voice."

He stood, bending and twisting to work out the night's stiffness. "Me, too. Well, we know it's there. And now we know it's traveling through a wall. Either we have a wandering spirit or we've got something with a real cause. Let's close down for the night and let the recorders do their work."

"Then?"

"I'm going to think hard about where that sound could be coming from and what could cause it. Because something sure as hell is."

CANDY WAS A bit shaken by having heard the voice. She hadn't expected to hear anything at all. Not a thing. She'd wanted to believe this was a wild-goose chase, even though they needed to help Vivian.

But how could they go to the parents and say that Vivian was hearing something real, but they couldn't solve the problem?

Although, according to Steve, he'd done that before. But she didn't believe that simply saying it was no threat would make Vivian feel any better. She was too young for that.

As they drove back to town, she glanced at the time. "Too late to try to sleep," she said, although she wanted to desperately.

"Same here. Maybe I'll go to the truck stop and load up on caffeine and an early breakfast."

"Mind if I join you?"

"I'd like that."

And he definitely would. "Your computer still searching?"

"It was when I left the office. Two possibilities. I want more."

"I can sure understand that. Maybe we can brainstorm our problem a bit."

Any excuse, she thought. She was strangely reluctant to leave Steve. Man, this was getting complicated, and about more than the Castelles.

She gave up. Changes were afoot inside her, and she didn't know how to stop them. She was just going to have to live with a hole deep inside when he left town.

The prospect was gloomy.

THE DINER WAS warm enough, but not hot. Long-haul trucks filled the parking lot, growling as drivers let them run. Maybe some were sleeping in their cabs. They might find it easier to drive on dark roads, but sleep made demands, too. Plus, they probably couldn't drive more than a certain number of hours at a stretch by law.

The diner, as well as warm enough, was busy. No doubt this was the time when the business made most of its money. They were surrounded by drivers digging into hearty breakfasts.

Which was exactly what Steve intended to do. Two sides of ham, for one. Four eggs. Four slices of toast, and something called a cheesy potato casserole.

Candy wasn't far behind in her order. Apparently being up all night made her hungry, too. She spread marmalade on her toast while he was content with the butter.

"Any ideas?" she asked. "We haven't discovered any

way that a human could get close enough to that house to make that voice."

"It's bothering you, huh?"

She frowned at her scrambled eggs. "Yeah, it is. I don't believe in woo-woo. That was…"

"Like woo-woo," he agreed. "I'd suggest a speaker of some kind, maybe automatically timed. But I think I'd have found something like that in the basement."

"Or in the wall?"

He shook his head. "I'm finding it hard to believe that a local electrician would have anything to do with that. Besides, they had the work done in their office. No joint wall with Vivian's room."

"That room kind of sticks out into nowhere," she remarked. "For myself I think I'd have used that for an office and given Vivian the office space."

"That's an idea. Maybe I'll suggest it if we can't find an answer." Now he frowned. "I can think of one person who might have put a speaker in a wall, and it's not an electrician."

"Todd."

He sighed and reached for his ham, beginning to slice it into mouth-sized pieces. "I've seen too much, Candy, but this is one I don't want to believe even though I've seen similar situations in the past."

"I hear you." She absolutely did. "Maybe we should have checked the office for the sounds."

"I'm certainly going to get around to it. At this point, though, I'm more worried about another agent. Now *that* could be a significant physical threat."

"What about a serious talk with Todd about his past?"

"Next on the menu. Maybe before the barn."

Candy nodded. "I think it's time."

Then he shocked her to her very core. "After this is over…"

She looked at him, waiting attentively.

"Man, I can't believe I'm going to be this boorish. Candy, I want you. But even more importantly, I want to get to know you. Really know you. You're like a puzzle box, and I want to turn the key."

She couldn't catch her breath. What was he saying? Sex was one thing, a dangerous thing, especially for women who tended to get emotionally involved. "I'm not a puzzle, Steve."

It was the only objection she could honestly offer.

"I'm not sure I meant it that way. Or maybe you are. But more and more I need to know you better outside this hunt. I'm fascinated."

Nobody had ever claimed to be fascinated by her before. Nor had anyone ever tried to get to know her much beyond the surface.

Her squad had known her as a soldier. They knew how much they could depend on her, what kind of fighter she was, but they'd never really gotten personal. Maybe because when you got to know someone under those circumstances, grief might not be far behind. Besides, the guys had been pretty much superficial with each other. Gab about letters from home, pictures of the kids. Sexual exploits.

Easy-to-share stuff.

Some of them had seemed to grow deeper friendships, but what had really mattered was the brotherhood, and she'd been invited inside it. She had become one of them.

But there were plenty of places none of them went, as far as she knew. Self-protection. Like the saying, *Don't get to know the FNGs*. The freaking new guys. Because they were inexperienced, they might be gone soon.

But now here was a guy who wanted to get past that point with her. She hadn't wanted to risk sex with him, but this was an even bigger risk.

She cleared her throat. "You'll be leaving in a couple of weeks."

"I'm talking about hanging around for a while. About building a friendship that can last longer than this job. Just think about it, if you can. If you don't want to…" He shrugged. "I'm a boor and you can just pretend I never said that."

Pretend was the right word for it, because it *would* be pretending. God, what to do now?

She honestly didn't know. All she knew was that with a few words he'd made her ache for a future she'd never believed would happen.

It also meant getting raw and exposed and vulnerable in ways she wasn't sure she could anymore.

"Thank you," she said finally and left it there. For safety's sake.

STEVE WANTED TO kick himself in the butt for pushing her that way. But there seemed to be no way to really get through to Candy that wasn't blunt. All the cards on the table where she could see them. Maybe no more suspicion about what he might want from her.

If she believed him, anyway.

Hell's bells. He'd never wanted to get that close to a woman, but now he did. A fling was one thing. This was no fling he was talking about. He didn't know where it might lead, if it ever happened, but with this woman he wanted to chance it.

After Candy left for the office and he settled on the bed in his motel room, he dragged his thoughts away from her and tossed around the Castelle case like a ball, one side to the other. Maybe mentally batting it against the wall.

He wanted to shake something out, but he still didn't have enough. He was by no means ready to ascribe all this to paranormal entities, residual energy or anything like that.

Proof. He always demanded it and hated it when he couldn't find any. There had been cases when all he could do was assure people they weren't in any danger. This time he couldn't even do that because of Todd's past.

Usually there was no measurable threat, just people who mainly wanted to be assured they weren't losing their minds. He understood that.

But this was different because of Vivian. There was no evidence that anyone or anything wanted to harm her physically, but that wasn't enough. She was being harmed in another way, a vital way.

Todd was willing to ditch the house and move. Steve would have given him props for that except it was possible that he knew how Annabelle would respond, knowing she wouldn't want to leave.

Or it might be that Todd didn't believe his past could be a threat. Also possible.

But then what? Damn, there were dried peas rattling around in this can somewhere and he needed to find one. Just one, to get him started in a useful direction.

But maybe he was already on that path and just hadn't pulled out the information that would show him.

A bedroom with nothing under it but a foundation

and a slab. Sounds he'd heard last night, sounds that Candy had heard, as well. Traveling through that wall as if it were wires to a phone.

He tended to discount the speaker idea, but he wasn't ready to throw that off the table. Nothing would be discarded until he knew he was clearly on track.

Dena was in an earlier time zone, so he wasn't especially surprised when she called him shortly after seven.

"Nothing on the street so far," she reported. "I'll keep feelers out, but you know these drug operations are pretty strong on secrecy. The Pentagon could learn something from them."

He didn't doubt it, he thought as he walked into the shower. To get anything out of these drug rings you had to plant someone on the inside. Difficult and dangerous. Then you had the problem of cops who fell into the dark side after living that life for so long. They closed up like clams.

First a talk with Todd, he decided. Then the barn. He had become fixated on it. If he could find evidence that someone was hiding in there…

Then what? How would the guy be scaring Vivian?

It was another stone to turn over. He was willing to turn stones over until his fingers were bloody. And then more.

He couldn't stop thinking about Vivian. About that little girl who needed to be rescued from something or someone.

No way was he going to leave her in a lurch.

IT WAS TEN before he phoned Candy, hoping she'd managed to get some sleep.

"Hey," she said.

Her voice didn't sound as if she'd slept much. Well, neither had he, and with another night investigation coming up, they needed to manage a few Zs somehow.

"Anything?" he asked.

"We'll see. I came up with more than a dozen Ivy Brides. Who would have thought the name would be that common. Anyway, more seem to still be popping up, so I'll let this run a while longer before I start investigating them individually."

He had no problem with that. "Wanna go with me soon?"

"Sure…"

Her voice trailed off. A ruckus sounded in the background and Candy cursed vigorously.

"I gotta go, Steve."

"What's up?"

"A repeat of the other day. Two more."

Now it was his turn to cuss. Two more? Hadn't Wittes said there'd be more?

But his primary reaction was feeling his stomach turn over and his mind kick into detective mode.

"Tell the sheriff my skills are available if he needs them."

"Sure." She disconnected.

God, he hoped she didn't have to go to the scene. Watching the video feed had messed her up enough.

He sat a while thinking about this. Two more murders. Maybe in keeping with the old lore? Tate had quoted the stories as saying there had been four murders.

A week before Halloween. Man, he'd be surprised if any parent let their youngsters go door-to-door.

Which always disappointed kids from what he'd

seen. The adventure of trick-or-treating vanished at a big party.

But now he'd have to deal with a frightened, possibly angry, town that had already focused on him, the outsider.

He swore again, torn between the two halves of himself: the cop and the TV host. No way he could do both.

And there was still a little girl who desperately needed help to return to a normal life.

But there were also two double murders, and since there'd been no major release of information on the first two, it was evident that the case hadn't been solved.

He was left wondering for the umpteenth time how humans could do this to each other. Stupid question. If he wondered, Candy could tell him.

Because that woman had seen it with her own eyes.

CANDY TRIED TO stay in the background. Watching the video had been troubling enough, but to have to go live to the scene... Well, she wondered how she'd handle it.

Yeah, she'd seen it in the Army, but that was in the past as much as she could shove it there. This might awaken the absolute worst of her nightmares.

But... She was a cop now. She'd have to face this sooner or later.

She stiffened herself, seeking her backbone. She could do it. She might have to.

Then Gage approached. "I'm a little shorthanded this morning."

Here it came.

"Who found them?" she asked, hoping her voice sounded steady. Or hard. She needed the hardening, and it was growing like ice within her.

"I've got four people out. One of them's sick. Another three left town on vacation. Mainly because I thought we'd be quiet for a while. We were hoping it was someone with a grudge. Nobody expected this to happen again."

"Why would anyone? Who found them?" she asked again.

"A couple of hunters. I expect they're being sick behind some trees."

She might do that, too.

"Candy…"

"I'll go out there." She heard the steel in her own voice. Combat mode was taking over.

"Thanks. If you get out there and feel it's too much, let me know. I can manage somehow."

But why should he? He'd given her this opportunity when no one else would. She didn't want to fail him. Not on a case as important as this.

"I'll be fine." She hoped. Then she added, "You know Steve Hawks's background. Former detective? He offered to help if you want him."

"I may need everyone I can get my hands on. Tell him he's on standby. This has to stop, and there's only one way."

CANDY DROVE OUT to the site, following her GPS. Her hands were steady on the wheel. The shakes and nausea had vanished for now. For now.

Why should Conard County be immune from the ugliness of people? Her vain hopes had been just that: vain. Now she was in the thick of it, and she knew how to manage. Later, after it was over, she might face other problems.

And she'd deal as she always had. Because she must.

Seeking refuge, she returned her thoughts to the Castelles. She hoped Steve continued his investigation for Vivian's sake. That little girl was still alive, unlike these latest victims. She deserved a kind of priority.

But her mind wouldn't let her off the hook for long. Instead she braced for the coming hours.

STEVE REALLY DIDN'T want to pursue the Castelle case. Not now. His internal tug-of-war was strengthening. Vivian, he reminded himself.

Somehow the Castelles had already heard about the murders. Maybe the grapevine had reached rapid-fire. Regardless of how they'd heard, they were visibly shaken.

Annabelle grabbed him as he came through the door. "You don't think… Vivian?"

"I don't see how these cases could be related." But he wasn't going to dismiss the possibility.

"Todd? I needed to talk to you privately." Might as well get this much out of the way.

"Sure," Todd answered. "Outside."

It was cold as hell out there this morning, but Steve agreed. He didn't want Annabelle or Vivian to hear any of this.

Out back, with Buddy running around like an over-grown demon, he faced Todd. "I need the truth from you, and I need it now."

For the first time Todd looked more than uneasy. He looked frightened.

Steve continued. "I heard about your drug conviction. Cocaine. Rehab."

Todd's nod was jerky. "Yeah. Rehab worked."

"Did it? Honestly? Look, I'm not a cop anymore, but I sure as hell need to know all the possibilities if I'm going to help your daughter."

Todd's gaze slid away. "Yeah, it worked. But maybe what worked more was Annabelle packing to leave and take Vivian with her. That's part of the reason we moved out here, to try to rebuild our marriage. I wasn't sure she'd ever forgive me. I'm still not convinced she has, at least not completely."

"Okay. I wondered. But there's something else."

Steve looked at him again.

"Did you leave the city while you owed someone money? Even a small amount." Because drug dealers sometimes made an example for even the smallest sums. Nobody was allowed to cheat them.

"I don't think so. I spent the last two years paying the guy off. It wasn't easy with the interest."

"Did they threaten you? Vivian? Annabelle?"

Todd shook his head. "I was paying them. They never said a word about my family."

Steve wasn't sure about that, even if it hadn't been explicitly stated. He sighed. Maybe this wasn't totally cleared up after all. Steve had needed a time-payment plan. This whole deck would be a lot cleaner if he had paid up front. But the odd thing about cocaine. It was expensive to begin with and as the need grew so did the cost.

"Okay," he said to Todd. "I won't mention it elsewhere."

At last Todd looked relieved. "Thanks."

Don't thank me too soon, he thought as he followed Todd back inside. He still had to recheck all his recording equipment in case he'd missed something.

He wondered if Candy would escape before he went to the barn. He might well need her help.

She'd become his right hand, and now he was glad his crew wasn't here. At this point he didn't need the confusion they'd bring.

But he might not have a show here at all.

And he didn't care.

CANDY WALKED TOWARD the bodies, her stride purposeful. She'd forgotten her qualms and was now focused. As in battle.

Never had she dreamed she'd need that mind-set again.

The area was roped off with crime scene tape. Men in clean suits were scouring the area around it. A weapon. They needed a weapon.

Candy looked at the two teens, a boy and a girl, and seriously doubted a weapon had been used. She knew what those kinds of wounds looked like. Too well.

"Looks like the same thing," Gage said.

She nodded. "They were drugged."

"How can you be sure?"

"I've seen everything any kind of weapon can do, from knives to guns to bombs. Unless you turn them over and find something, I have to conclude they were drugged before they were brought here."

Gage nodded. "The thought had crossed my mind."

"Were they an item?"

"I believe so. I seem to remember them dating."

"Probably. Else why take them both? Any toxicology on the first two?"

"Not yet.

"Hell." She stared, her feelings silenced. "What are you going to do?"

"You mean apart from the investigation? Plant posters and warnings all over town. Take your kids to the party at the high school or keep them home."

"Good idea. I'd assume at this point, though, that the very young kids would be safe."

"But that's not a reliable assumption. I'll get the teens who are staging the party to set a room aside for the little ones. Maybe soften the haunted house. I'm sure they will, under the circumstances."

Candy nodded, using her eyes to seek more information. Then the techs arrived with their yellow numbered markers. Someone called out that he'd found a trail that looked as if the kids had been dragged.

A drag trail. That fit with Candy's idea of drugs. But how? "I hope they'll check stomach contents."

Gage nodded. "That's one thing we can do here."

"But not the toxicology?"

"Not complete enough. There are some things the local hospital can't look for. Not yet anyway. Not enough call for it."

Candy understood, but she sighed anyway. Waiting on information wouldn't prevent another set of murders. They needed to find the killer.

Just as Steve needed to find a perp so he could help Vivian.

STEVE SET ABOUT reviewing all his equipment for any signs that someone had been in this house. Or that a spook had been making noise.

Several hours later he had nothing except the faint sounds coming up the wall that both he and Candy had heard. He didn't want to tell that to the Castelles, because it would only confirm their ideas about the paranormal.

Not yet. He needed more before he fell back on that. Much more than rhythms of speech coming through that wall.

He decided to leave all his equipment in place, then saw Ben Wittes in the driveway. Oh, for God's sake. Like he needed that idiot right now.

But Annabelle let him in anyway. Steve met him in the hallway. "What's up?"

"I told you there'd be more murders. My spirit guide says it's the guy who killed his wife. Talking. Mumbling."

Steve wanted to sigh. Nothing there. Finally he busted the guy's bubble. "You need to tell me something that isn't part of the legends that appear to have been created by local kids years ago. No real murders showed up in police reports back then."

Ben closed his eyes, then snapped them open. "Maybe they didn't find the victims. Or maybe he wasn't strong enough to do it back then. He's strong enough now."

Steve heard a small sound behind him and swung around to see Vivian hiding behind her mother, her face peeping out and looking terrified.

"That does it," he said. "Vivian doesn't want you here. You're fired. And if you come back, no one will let you in this house. You understand?"

Fury flickered across Ben Wittes's face, then vanished.

"If that's the way you want it," he grumbled. "But you'll be sorry if you miss more information."

"You haven't provided one useful thing. If you think you've got something better, then find me in town. Now go."

Steve was surprised at the amount of relief he felt as Wittes disappeared down the driveway.

He turned to look at Annabelle and Vivian.

"Are you sure that was wise?" Annabelle asked.

"He offered nothing that I wasn't able to find out from the old sheriff. Besides—" he squatted and spoke to Vivian "—you didn't like him, did you?"

She shook her head. Then she did something that tore his heart. She put her thumb in her mouth.

"I promise he won't come back."

"Good," Vivian said around her thumb. "Buddy."

Annabelle spoke. "He's out back, honey. Want him inside?"

Buddy came charging in, apparently glad of the warm temperature. Well, yeah. That dog had an awfully short coat. Maybe that was why he'd been running nonstop out there.

Vivian went to the kitchen table, forgetting her thumb. "Chocolate," she said firmly.

Annabelle smiled. "I should take out stock in the instant cocoa business."

"Sounds like a great idea," Steve said cheerfully. "I'm going to take a look at your barn, if that's okay?"

"Go ahead," Annabelle answered.

And where had Todd gone? Steve wondered. Had he just disappeared because Steve had raked up bad memories? Or because he hadn't been honest with the whole story?

Hell, there was no way to know if the guy simply wouldn't tell him.

Frustrated, Steve headed out to the barn. Waste of his time, probably, but no stone left unturned. A major rule of his life.

CANDY RETURNED HOME around seven in the evening. She'd picked up a sandwich for dinner but had no desire to eat it. Habit had made her buy it. Not even habit could make her eat right then.

It was hitting her, she realized. Damn, she had feared this, but there was no way to stop it now. She had been cast back into places she never wanted to go again, and now those memories were swimming with memories of what she had seen today.

More hideous reality. Would she never escape it?

But the wish vanished in the memories. She began to shake. Had to run to vomit. Returned to her kitchen on shaky legs and tried to make coffee but dropped the pot twice and gave up.

Then she collapsed at the table and let the sobbing begin. Tears, so many tears, some of them unshed for so long that they demanded to join the outpouring.

Maybe she was in the wrong job after all. But she recoiled from that idea. Where would she go? What would she do?

She felt trapped in past and present, unable to live with herself, unable to do anything else. She couldn't quit. She wasn't a quitter, and whenever suicide tried to drift through her mind, she tossed it away much more easily than memory.

Those kids. Those poor kids. But how many other kids had she seen die? Eighteen-year-olds wearing the same uniform as hers. Others, as young as ten or twelve in raggedy clothes, dead because they'd been in the wrong place.

Too many kids by far. She couldn't fight it any longer. Memory was taking over and everything else disappeared.

She even smelled gunpowder. Heard explosions and gunfire. She was back in the 'Stan now with more kids riding her shoulders. The weight threatened to crush her.

She hardly heard a familiar voice say, "The door was open..."

Then Steve's strong arms surrounded her tightly. Hanging on to her as if he wanted to stop her fall. But nothing could. Nothing.

One of those big hands stroked her hair but she was hardly aware of it. Lost within herself, she couldn't find a way out.

She continued sobbing.

STEVE SWEPT HER up in his arms when he felt her soften just a bit and carried her to her bed. Then, lying beside her, he felt her soak his shirt with her tears, felt the tremors run through her. Could almost feel the memories that were swamping her.

Though he had some himself that would never leave him, he knew they were nothing like Candy's. If ever he'd wished for a magic wand, he did now.

And he hated wars because they did this to people. All people.

A LONG TIME LATER, Candy's tears dried, and her body stopped shaking. He was relieved when she fell asleep.

He wouldn't leave, though. She was going to wake feeling fragile, and he refused to disturb her sleep.

Sleep was healing, and she needed every bit of it she could get.

He wished he knew if being a cop might eventually desensitize her to memories. Like immersion therapy. Afraid of spiders? Then look at dozens of photos of spiders. Then observe them for real. Maybe eventually let them crawl on you.

But it probably wouldn't, he decided. This wasn't like spiders or anything similar. This was a great gaping wound in her psyche. A little spackle and paint wouldn't patch it.

A grim prospect. He had to hope that time would help her heal. But she'd been doing pretty well so far. She'd landed a job, she appeared to be functioning in it.

Then there was today. He bet she'd gone out to the murder scene this time. Because at her very core she was tough. Tough as steel.

He liked the woman he knew now. But he damn well admired her strength, especially given where she'd been.

She didn't want to see her family for fear of the questions they would ask, worried that they'd see how much she had changed and would start poking around.

Well, that sounded like a good family, the kind he'd like. Someone just needed to suggest to them that they ought to stay away from anything she didn't mention herself.

That thing about feeling responsible for her brother's death really cut at him, though. She didn't deserve to feel that way, and her brother most decidedly didn't deserve it. Give the guy his due for choosing to enlist. Candy hadn't held him at gunpoint.

But how could anyone convince her of that? Guilt didn't yield to logic. Ever.

He closed his eyes, enjoying having her tucked up against him. He wondered if she'd ever open up to him, a prerequisite for any deep relationship, even friendship.

That was a decision she had to make for herself,

however. She had to come to trust him enough, and he couldn't see any way to make that happen.

Sleep crept up on him at last, carrying him away into a world of confusing dreams that were half born of the Castelle situation, half born of his concerns for Candy, and the rest, around the edges, about four hideous murders.

Even sleep didn't offer him real escape.

STEVE AWOKE WHILE it was still dark outside, not that it meant much at this time of year, not in these parts anyway.

Candy had slipped away. He could smell soaps and shampoos and feel humidity: a shower. That sounded good to him, too, but pointless. He didn't have a change of clothing.

More important, he wanted to see Candy, to see if she was doing better now.

The aroma of coffee pulled him down the hallway to the kitchen. The pot, still mostly full, issued an invitation. After he filled a mug, he went looking and found Candy seated in the living room, her feet up on a sofa, staring into space.

Keeping quiet, he sat in a chair across from her. She'd speak when she was ready. Or not.

She looked like hell, though. The dark circles under her eyes announced the rough night she'd had.

She spoke at last. "You must need to get to work."

Was that a suggestion that he should leave? If so, he was in no mood to listen. Not when she looked like that. The Castelles could damn well wait a few hours.

He decided to speak, choosing to focus on his work. It seemed like the only safe topic right now.

"I fired the psychic yesterday."

Her gaze found him. "Really? I thought you couldn't."

"I have *some* pull," he answered. "It's *my* show, after all. They give me too much trouble, I walk. Believe me, I know how to walk away."

She nodded wearily. "I guess you do."

Except from her. Stubbornly, he stayed where he was. "You got any time today?"

"All day. Gage told me not to come in. But he didn't tell me not to do my liaising with you."

"So you work anyway." Better for her than thinking about dead kids. Gage was right about that. The man must be pretty good at judging the emotional state of his deputies.

"Yeah," she answered listlessly. "Why'd you fire Wittes?"

"Because he sounds like a rerun of the lore Tate told us about. Nothing new, just a story that may or may not unjustly accuse a man no one even remembers now. Pretty rotten eulogy, if you ask me."

"I agree."

"But he wasn't the only reason. He scared Vivian."

She appeared to be fully reentering the present. "I'm not surprised, Steve. He'd scare any little kid, and some adults."

"No kidding." He sipped his cooling coffee, ignoring the loss of heat. Hers must have reached room temperature by now, but even though he could have refilled their mugs, he decided not to. All that seemed to be pulling her back from the precipice was focusing on something safe...like his ghost hunt.

Ha. Safe? This whole thing was beginning to appear less safe by the hour. His cop senses had gone on full alert.

"I'm not sure those murders aren't related to the Castelle situation." Damn! Bad timing to bring up the killings. Where was his head at? The wrong place. He'd evidently lost some caution in the years since he'd quit his department.

But she didn't withdraw, didn't pull into herself. Her gaze had become clearer. The night's storm seemed to have passed for now.

"You're giving me chills," she remarked. "I need more coffee. Hot this time."

"I could run out and get us lattes, if you want." Much as he didn't want to leave her, he'd have crawled over glass to do just one thing to make her feel that someone cared. To make her feel even a tiny bit better.

It shook him a little to realize he'd seldom cared that much for another person. Willing to give the shirt off his back, but to crawl on glass? Oh, he had it bad.

She smiled slightly. "I'd like that, if you don't mind."

He rose. "I don't mind at all. What about breakfast? I'm sure Maude will dish up something good. Anything in particular?"

"Her home fries. I seem to be craving carbs."

"I'm not surprised." Not at all. That kind of stress, or even shock, required something to pump the blood sugar up.

He pulled on his jacket, not caring how scruffy he probably looked by now. Showering and changing could wait for a better time. He figured he must be breaking the town's speed limit on his way to the diner.

But it was still early, and there were few cars on the

road. Maude's seemed to have just opened, and only a handful people sat scattered among the tables.

"I heard," Maude said to him across the counter.

"Yeah. Candy's…well."

Maude nodded. "Ex-soldier, now this. Not what she expected from this job. Load her up?"

"She specifically mentioned your home fries."

Maude frowned, which he was learning to recognize as her smile. "And more," she said decisively. "You, too?"

"Filling the tanks," he agreed.

He left with four foam containers instead of the two he'd expected, and four extralarge lattes. Maude signaled one of the breakfast customers. "Help Steve here out to his car. Don't want them lattes spilling. They're for Candy."

Making it even more clear this was caretaking. The guy she had called over smiled faintly. "You betcha. Gotta take care of that girl."

"Girl?" Maude snorted. "She's done more in her life than you'd ever want to see, Bill. She ain't no *girl*."

Steve wanted to applaud, but Maude didn't seem like the right woman to applaud. Bill helped him get everything safely stashed in his rental, an achievement with all that coffee. Then Steve was driving back, this time at a sane pace.

It took him three trips, but he put all the bounty on the kitchen table. Candy emerged from the living room and looked at everything. "Did you rob her?"

"Maude made up the order. Was I going to argue? I bet one of her glares could turn me to ash."

That drew an almost natural smile from Candy. She

reached first for a coffee and swallowed half of it before at last taking a seat.

Steve, meanwhile, opened the containers, revealing enough fried potatoes to feed a small army, followed by a load of scrambled eggs with a stack of bacon, then generous slices of pineapple with a side of cherries. And finally a container filled with some kind of coffee cake.

"Fit for a king," he remarked as he gathered up utensils and plates. "Dig in."

She finished the first latte, so he pushed a second toward her.

"Want a shot of whiskey in that?"

Her gaze rose to his face. "Do you have any?" She sounded surprised.

"Hell no, but I always thought it would be cool to carry a flask."

Another smile, a small sound that might have been an attempt to laugh. She was taking her first steps toward relaxing. He was delighted to see her reaching for potatoes, fruit and bacon. The eggs didn't seem to interest her, but he could take care of that himself.

She spoke when she'd made a remarkable dent on breakfast. "You have plans for today?"

"Absolutely. Join me, please. I've got more tapes and recordings to run through, and I'm thinking about a second walk-through with my infrared camera. Then there's the barn. I did a quick scan yesterday, but a second pair of eyes would be helpful, if you're willing."

She nodded, eating another slice of pineapple before taking a piece of coffee cake. "That barn keeps drawing your attention. Are you sure you're not obsessed?"

"Who, me? No, it's just that it seems like a good hiding place. I need to explore it for signs someone might have been hanging around in there."

"Reasonable." She put her fork down. "I've overdone it. I don't think I'll want to eat for a week."

That made him laugh. "You want me to bet on that?"

She looked almost sheepish. "I had a lot of training in *eat when you can because you don't know when you'll get another chance.*"

"I believe it. It's good to see you filling up, though. And I'm catching up."

"Do you work out a lot to keep that figure?"

Well, that was the most personal thing she'd ever said to him. He liked it. "Some. I don't overdo it, though. Doing it for health is one reason. Doing it for show is another."

He cleaned up when they were done, not a difficult task. A few items in the dishwasher, a few leftovers in the fridge.

"Ready to go?" he asked.

Chapter Fourteen

Candy didn't wear her uniform. She sat beside Steve in jeans, a yellow sweater and a quilted jacket. Leather gloves protected her hands.

"What's first?" she asked. "Barn? House?"

"I see clouds on the horizon, so I want to do the barn first, while we still have decent light."

Winter had stolen the last color from the landscape, and the cold ground crunched under their feet as Steve began to pull some industrial-sized flashlights from his trunk.

"Want one?" he asked.

"Oh, come on." She liked his impish smile. Heck, she liked a lot about him, mostly that he hadn't just run last night. She wouldn't have blamed him if he had.

A lot of people couldn't handle her episodes. She'd learned that the hard way, losing friends she'd made since her discharge. She hadn't lost any here yet, but then they hadn't seen her the way Steve had seen her last night. She was just glad she hadn't flown into a rage, something that happened occasionally. Rarely, but it *did* happen.

Steve stuck his head in the house to tell the Castelles what they were doing. Candy half expected Todd to follow them, but he didn't.

"There was more mumbling," Steve said as he joined her on the walk to the barn. "Vivian's still upset."

"She wasn't in her room, was she?"

"No, in the hallway early this morning. On her way to the bathroom."

"Damn. That kid ought to be able to go to the bathroom without terror."

"You'd think."

Light filtered through loose slats in the barn, beams that bounced off enough dust to make them visible.

"Dang," Candy said. "Was it windy last night? What stirred up all this dust?"

Steve simply looked at her and she got the message. No ghost should do that.

A familiar uneasiness began to creep up her spine to her neck. *Hostiles.* Then she caught herself. Overreaction.

Steve spoke. "Let's start toward the back. When we get halfway through, we can climb the ladders to the hayloft and check around."

The loft might be the most dangerous place in this barn if anyone was here.

Candy's backbone was stiffening again. She could feel it. Rising to the demands of the moment. If she'd brought one good thing back from the war, that was it.

The back of the barn wasn't all that interesting. A tack room empty of everything except a ragged halter that at a touch felt too dried out and stiff to ever be used again.

She let go of it, then moved forward with Steve, checking every possible nook, even the decrepit horse stalls. Easy to imagine what this place had once looked like. Filled with horses and hay and other feed. People coming and going. The scent of horses, strangely enough, seemed to linger even after many years.

The loft was still covered with some loose hay. A fire hazard, she thought, but no signs of recent disturbance. Not up here anyway. Then back down and a sweep of the front of the barn. Several times she looked upward because she didn't trust the roof. It sagged too much.

Then her foot snagged on something. A loose board? But when she looked down she saw an old cut.

"Steve? Come take a look at this."

He hurried over, squatting down to peer at the place she indicated with the wide beam of her light.

"That's curious." He straightened and looked around. "My kingdom for some kind of broom."

But Candy was already using her foot to sweep hay and other detritus from the area. The dust in the barn was getting thick. Thick and flammable. She didn't stop and Steve joined her.

Then, with a sweep of his foot, he revealed a large iron ring. He looked at Candy.

"A trapdoor," she said.

Steve stared down again. "It sure looks like one."

He pulled it open, up and back. If they'd expected to find storage, they discovered it empty except for gray boards lining parts of it. Both shined their lights into a dark hole that appeared ten feet deep. The only thing inside it was a handmade ladder, the wood old.

"Weird," Candy said.

"No, look." Excitement crept into Steve's voice. He pointed his light again. "There's a tunnel."

Five minutes later, Steve climbed down into the hole over Candy's strong objections.

"It could collapse on you! Who knows how old this is? Can you trust those ancient boards?"

His expression said he would not be deterred. "You're here to call for help if anything happens. But Candy, this could explain so much. This could be where the voice is coming from."

"I'll allow that, but how do you know someone isn't waiting down there? You could get into all kinds of trouble."

"It's possible, but not likely. If it'll make you feel any better, we'll sit here listening. If we don't hear anything, I'm going in."

That didn't make her feel one whit better, but she knew when she was running into a brick wall. She gave up arguing. Maybe the boards were strong enough to hold it.

Eventually, Steve refused to wait any longer. "My GPS says the tunnel heads toward the house."

Candy stiffened. God in heaven. Had he found the problem? But then, who might it be? She forced herself to calm down. There was no indication this tunnel ran all the way to the house. Why would it?

Besides, those boards looked too old to have been added recently. Way too old. Maybe there'd been some mining in the past? There were certainly enough old tunnels up on Thunder Mountain to the west.

And now she knew why Steve wore a watch. She hadn't paid it much mind, thinking it was one of those fitness things. Apparently it did more than count his footsteps. GPS. Maybe a compass. Always prepared.

By the beam of her flashlight, and his, she watched

him disappear into the dark opening. After a bit, his flashlight diminished, illuminating little from her point of view.

If he went too far, she doubted she'd be able to get him help in time if that tunnel collapsed. Damn, she should never have let him go in alone. Ten or fifteen feet apart might have made one or the other of them much safer, more likely to be able to crawl out for help.

Or not. They might both be sealed in a tomb of tumbling earth and rocks.

Then Steve's head popped out of the tunnel. "There are some fresh boards in here, and something walled off at the end of the tunnel."

"I'm coming in."

"Seems safe enough." He didn't try to dissuade her, which was good. Hanging around as the protected woman didn't suit her at all.

Moving carefully, she climbed down the old boards, feeling them give a little, but not enough to worry her. These timbers were thick, not simple two-by-fours.

Mining timbers, she thought. An old mine. What good could it be now?

In places she had to crawl, scuffing her knees some despite her jeans. Curiosity drove her forward, following Steve, carrying her own flashlight.

It got dark in a tunnel. Way dark. She was grateful for the beams that stretched a lighted path in front of her.

Steve called out quietly. "There seems to be a wall ahead."

Ten minutes later, they reached the wall he was talking about. She scanned it as he said, "Those are fresh timbers."

She agreed. Water had only just started to darken them.

"Who would…?" She didn't bother to finish the question. Pointless.

Then memory climbed up her throat. "I crawled through tunnels like this in Afghanistan."

His head swiveled to look at her. "You need to get out?"

"No. I made it before, I can do it now. I just wish I had a grenade."

That drew a hollow laugh from him. "I hear you."

Maybe he did. Or her rifle, not that it would make crawling through here any easier. Nah, a grenade.

Unexpectedly, the idea amused her. Some habits died hard, she guessed.

They sat staring at the wall before them.

"It's new," he repeated. "And if my measurements are correct, this may reach under Vivian's bedroom."

She caught her breath. "We've got to get past this. See what's going on."

"Start looking. I'm not too keen on just randomly removing these timbers. If someone is using it, there has to be a way inside."

"Yeah." Candy started running her light around the edges. Good place to begin, she thought. A crumble of dirt from above her head fell and struck her on the back. Her breath nearly stopped in her throat.

But Steve had already rolled on his back, pointing his light upward. "Doesn't seem like much to worry about. A little drying soil. The rest of the timbers look okay."

She wondered about the person or people who had built this tunnel. A lot of work, and those timbers had to be carted in from somewhere else. A heap of determination, but she couldn't imagine the purpose unless somebody had discovered something valuable.

Gold may have washed down from the mountains. Some still did, but not enough to make anyone rich. Silver, too, at times. She'd also seen a lot of tunnels closed off with the radiation trefoil warning. A lot of deadly things were buried deep in the earth, things never meant to be brought above ground in appreciable quantities.

Look at those tailing piles outside the old mining town on Thunder Mountain. To this day, nothing grew on them. She had to wonder what toxic heavy metals were washing down from them into the groundwater, into streams.

Frequent water checks around the town apparently said local water was safe. She wondered, sometimes, if they were accurate.

"Look at this," she said, her gaze suddenly fixing on a narrow line, like a fine cut, finer than the one in the barn floor.

"Damn, your eyes are good."

"Situational awareness," she had briefly. It had never left her.

Steve tapped on it. "It's not that thick."

"I don't see any hinges. Maybe it pulls out?"

He began to test around the edges. He wasn't wearing gloves, so he could feel better. She wasn't ready to ditch her own. It was damn cold down here. Not warmer the way most things underground were, but cold as ice. Her cheeks ached from it.

"There," he said. "A divot, just enough to grip with fingers. You ready?"

"For what? Of course I'm ready. I'm here."

Reaching out, he searched farther. "There we are. A door in this wall."

Her heart had begun to gallop. What were they going to find in there? Nothing good, she suspected.

She reached out to help Steve as he pulled the panel free. Another dark hole greeted them. Light didn't make it look much better.

They crawled in, Steve leading, then he cursed.

"What?"

"I think it's a freaking bomb shelter."

"Wow." She crawled in beside him, scanning the area with her light. Bunks. Water containers. Shelves full of canned foods that had begun to rust. "Another era."

"No kidding. But why an entry out in the barn?"

"Ask the builder," she said drily.

Then everything inside her froze. "Steve? Steve, is that a coffin?"

STEVE NOW SAW IT, too. Under the bottom bunk. Made roughly of boards like the ones outside. Strangely dust free.

"It looks like one," he agreed. "God. What did we find?"

"Ivy Bride?"

"Ghoulish," he said flatly.

"Don't touch it," she said sharply. "It's time to call for some help."

"Like the sheriff isn't busy enough?"

"It doesn't matter. There are laws against disturbing human remains. You know that, Steve."

He nodded. Of course he knew it. Besides, if there was a body in there, he didn't want to destroy any evidence. Nor would he and Candy learn a thing even if they looked. His detective cap, however, seemed to be pinching his skull.

"Let's go," he said. "We should guard the entry."

Gage arrived twenty minutes later. "You should have called us before you crawled into the tunnel," Gage said when he joined them above ground with four deputies. "Steve, you know better than that."

Steve frowned. "We didn't expect to find anything like that. Dang, Gage, we were just looking for signs that someone might be under Vivian's room making the voices she heard. If that's all we found, we would have still called you. But this?" He shook his head. "Never would have expected it in a million years."

BEN WITTES WATCHED from the distance, the voice in his head growing louder.

They found it. At last.

"What you talkin' about?" Ben demanded of the spirit. "You killed her."

No. I didn't. I just couldn't let go.

Now Ben was truly disturbed. What had he been used for? Why did the spirit want this? What about the angry woman?

"What about the kids killed on the mountain?" Ben demanded of the voice. "You did that."

No.

Just that. *No.* Ben grabbed his head, wanting to crush it with his own hands. He was so confused. So overwhelmed. He couldn't begin to explain it. He just wished it would stop. He didn't want to hear these voices. He didn't *want* to know these things. Why were the spirits tormenting him this way? What had he ever done?

Why had he spent so many nights at the direction of this damn voice sitting down there and talking to that coffin? Singing to it?

To make a dead man happier?

"Go away," Ben said forcefully. "Go now."

The voice laughed. *I'm not done with you yet.*

What the hell did that mean?

Forgetting that he wanted to watch the sheriff uncover all this stuff, he took off running.

Then the voice again. *Find me some more kids.*

No, Ben screamed in his mind. *No!*

He didn't even understand what the spirit meant, but it horrified him.

Wafting up into his terrified brain came memories of waking in the morning covered with dirt. The tunnel? Or something worse?

BY FOUR THAT AFTERNOON, the sheriff's team had pulled the coffin out of its hiding place. Techs crawled everywhere seeking evidence. The bodies on the mountain were going to have to wait awhile.

Steve stood staring into the distance, Candy nearby as she took notes and answered questions.

Two kids. Four now. An old coffin. How could all of this be linked? Because his finely tuned senses told him none of this was coincidence. The voices had been explained, and soon he'd be able to reassure Viv.

But not before this damned coffin was gone. Not until they knew why someone had been sitting down there babysitting that thing.

No true answers until then.

Chapter Fifteen

The last thing Candy and Steve heard about that coffin was that it contained bones. Nothing but bones. Well, Steve thought, that wouldn't reveal much but a medical examiner could find more.

With Halloween two days away, it was sad to see the streets so empty. Local radio had been advising people to take their children to the party at the high school. Posters plastered every light post and flat surface around town.

And not one person had placed a candle in a pumpkin.

The night was growing cold, clouding over with the possibility of snow or rain. An unwelcoming night.

He'd reviewed all the evidence he had from the Castelle house and couldn't even answer their questions about what had happened in the barn. The sheriff's presence had raised plenty of questions for them, but at least they didn't seem to think it could be related in any way to the voices Vivian heard.

Good enough for now.

At nine that night, his cell phone rang. Candy. Her voice sounded as tight as a coiled spring.

"Steve, two more teens have gone missing. We're starting a search on the mountain immediately."

"How long have they been gone?"

"Since shortly after school let out."

Still time, he thought. Still time. "I'm coming, too."

"I'll pick you up."

SHE ROLLED UP in front of the motel, and he was waiting, ready. A heavier jacket this time, gloves, knit cap.

"We've got to find them," she said tensely.

"Alive," he agreed. "At least we've got a general idea of where to look."

Small comfort, she thought. At least these kids hadn't been missing for that long. The others had taken way too long to find. Maybe not this pair.

"Boy and girl?" he asked.

"Yeah. From what I've heard, they decided to walk home from school. Out of town. They both live on ranches, but the houses aren't more than a couple miles from the high school."

"I used to do things like that. It was always fun to be with my girlfriend where no one would bother us."

Candy spoke after a minute or two. "I had a duenna."

He turned on the seat. "Seriously?"

"My family is old-fashioned in some ways. Now that I'm older, I see it differently. Everywhere I went I had protection. My aunt seemed to love it. She visited places she might never have gone otherwise. Heck, at the arcade she got into one of the games. Sometimes I thought I wouldn't be able to pry her away."

"Sounds like a wonderful aunt." Dating must have been difficult, though.

"She was. She always seemed to enjoy watching over me, as if it were a great adventure."

"Maybe for her it was like being a teen again."

"Maybe. I know I chafed at it."

The road had started to climb steeply, then they saw the lights ahead. Flood lamps, flashlights moving through the trees.

Gage stood at a command center, directing the search parties. Radios crackled constantly. Two ambulances stood ready. It looked like half the county had turned out for this one. Just from where Candy stood, she reckoned there were maybe a hundred searchers moving about three feet apart. A good sweep.

She just hoped the teens hadn't been tied up a long distance away.

There was no longer any doubt in anyone's mind what they were looking for. A third case. The first two had set a precedent, but this one would confirm it beyond any doubt.

They had a serial killer.

TWO HOURS LATER, Candy and Steve heard a faint cry. She took off like a bat out of hell in that direction. Steve dashed after her. Candy's flashlight swept back and forth as she looked out for obstacles or unexpected ravines. He followed suit.

Candy paused, calling out the names of the two students. "Mark? Mabs?"

Again a faint cry, louder this time. A crashing behind them announced that other searchers were on their way. Ten minutes later they reached the two teens, tied to trees facing each other. Cold. Drugged. Only Mabs was awake enough to cry out.

Very soon the medics arrived and survival blankets wrapped the extremely cold pair. A short time later they were carted out of the woods on stretchers.

It was nearly midnight.

On the walk back to the car, Steve said, "I need to get out to the Castelles."

"Why? They must be sleeping by now."

He shook his head. "Candy, someone was in that tunnel. Now six teens have been kidnapped. There's a very strong part of me that can't believe none of this is related. Too much weirdness."

She had to acknowledge that he might be correct. What's more, all the department's activity at the tunnel had ceased when word of the kids' disappearance had reached them. An old coffin containing bones hardly seemed like an emergency.

"I'll go with," she said. Because the feeling had begun to grow in her, as well. A mind that was capable of treating those teens that way was capable of harming Vivian. Urgency rode her as she drove as quickly as she dared toward the Castelles' house.

"Thank God those kids were okay," she remarked. As if they'd ever be okay again. Not after something like that.

Steve's response was short. "They're alive at least."

Consolation, for what it was worth. "You think it could have something to do with Todd's past?"

"I don't know what he might have been withholding. I could hardly threaten him."

Questions plagued her. Drug dealers? She supposed it was possible. Easier to think about than some sicko who'd been walking the streets of this town all his life.

Steve spoke. "Is Candy Serrano your full name?"

What had brought that on? she wondered. "Actually, it's Candela de Serrano."

"That's pretty."

"I've been shortening it since middle school. Candle of the Mountains may have appealed to my parents, but it always seemed like a whole mouthful to me."

"I hope you didn't shorten it because of your heritage. It's beautiful. I just wondered."

Anything to keep from thinking about the danger they might have left behind them at the Castelles'. Never had this drive felt so long.

As soon as they pulled into the driveway, Steve leaped out, running for the front door. Candy, feeling his urgency, pulled her gun belt and service pistol out of her locked trunk and tightened them around her waist. Then she took off after Steve.

She arrived at the door in time to see a harried Todd open it. The instant he spied Steve, he said, "The voice again. And this time I heard it, too."

Damn, Candy thought, her insides tightening. Someone had to be down in that tunnel.

"It sounds like he might be screaming," Todd added. He stepped back, opening the door wide.

"Stay here," Steve said. "Lock the doors."

Todd's eyes widened, his mouth opened, then closed. "What?"

Candy spoke. "Todd, please. Get together and lock up. This might be no ghost at all."

Todd nodded jerkily as if trying to absorb all of it. "That's why the sheriff was out back earlier?"

"It's possible," Steve said. "Just let us check it out."

As they strode toward the barn, Candy said, "I'm calling for backup."

He didn't argue. They were both fairly certain now that there could be a man in that tunnel. Possibly upset about the missing coffin.

Possibly armed. Likely a serious threat if he was involved with those teens.

Candy felt that uneasy prickle again, the sense of impending danger. Like a night patrol, when the enemy could be hard to see even with night vision goggles. Plenty of impenetrable things to hide behind.

This guy had a tunnel. Concealment. No, he couldn't get past them on his way out, or at least she thought he couldn't, unless there was a door they'd missed. But they'd be every bit as trapped as he was.

Glancing at Steve, she decided he was going into his own type of combat mode. Maybe from his street days. There was little light to see by, except what reached them from the house. The clouds had begun to dump sleet.

Thank God they had found those teens before the icy weather had done its work.

They both crept into the barn, aware that any noise they made might be heard below. Impossible to know how much sound the tunnel would deaden.

They found the trapdoor open. They shared a look in the darkness and listened. They heard a voice rambling from deep inside. Not very loud.

"They took you away, my love. I'm so sorry I couldn't stop them."

"Damn," Steve whispered. "I could swear that's Ben Wittes."

"Yeah. I'll go down first."

"But…"

"I'm armed. Quit being a *guy*." She had the feeling

that he might have laughed under other circumstances. Regardless, unlike him she had faced situations like this.

She slipped down into the hole, wincing as the nylon of her jacket rubbed against the boards. Loud to her ears, but the voice from down the tunnel didn't stop.

Kneeling, she began to make her way through the tunnel. It dipped down a little just past the entrance, but not enough to cause a problem. There was, however, more detritus on the floor. Rocks, dirt, all the things dislodged by the people who'd recovered the coffin and spent hours logging any evidence they could find.

As her knee hit a sharp rock, she wanted to cuss. Then she heard Steve moving behind her. No light, no light at all so as not to warn their quarry of their approach. Feeling her way along slowed her down, but it didn't matter. She'd crept slower through worse. At least she'd been in this tunnel before.

Then she saw a glimmer of light ahead. It appeared their quarry had placed the panel over the door, but not fitted it tightly. So maybe the tunnel had amplified his voice?

No, not at all. He was talking and singing loudly now, switching from a lullaby to talk. When he talked he sounded furious, then soothing.

"You're still here," he said. "Sam knows it. Damn those people who took you out of here. Sam wants me to kill them all. And maybe I will." A pause. "I got a gun, Ivy. To make it happen faster."

Hell, Candy thought. She wished she could look over her shoulder and find out if Steve had heard, but it was still so dark in here, despite the little bits of light that worked their way around the panel.

Moving as silently as she could, she unsnapped her holster and drew out her pistol. The faintest click as she released the safety.

A steely, familiar calm settled over her. When she pulled that panel down, she'd have to move fast. Wittes might have that gun he'd mentioned near at hand. She wished she'd taken time to don the body armor that was in the trunk of her car.

Idiotic. But too late.

Candy drew a deep breath, worked her fingers around the edge of the panel and threw it to one side.

"You thought I didn't hear you? Sam knew you were coming."

She stared straight into the barrel of a shotgun.

STEVE SAW THE shotgun over Candy's shoulder. He had enough experience to know what the dispersal of that shot would do to her. He eased forward, trying to figure out how to help. Her pistol was out of his reach. God. He had to find a way.

But experience helped Candy react. She flattened and rolled to one side, out of range.

Startled, Ben tried to follow her with his gun, which gave Steve the opportunity he needed. He launched forward, difficult to do from a prone position, but he managed it, again startling Ben, who didn't seem to know how to handle this.

Ben swung his gun around toward Steve. Candy aimed her pistol and fired, missing Ben.

"You'll never get out of here," Steve growled. "Sheriff's waiting at the head of the tunnel. Don't be stupid and shoot an officer."

Candy, who'd rolled over again with her pistol aimed, ready to shoot, stopped herself.

Steve watched the most amazing thing happen. He saw Ben start to deflate, almost as if he were a balloon. Sagging, shrinking in on himself, looking confused.

The shotgun dropped. Ben stared at it as if he couldn't understand. Then the man looked at them as if seeing them for the first time.

It took only a moment for the two of them to wrestle Ben to the ground. Candy had zip ties on her utility belt, and used them swiftly on Ben's wrists, while Steve crawled into the shelter and moved the shotgun safely away, opening it to remove the load.

"Done," he said. "Now we just have to figure out how to get him out of here."

Candy turned her head to Steve. "What just happened?"

"Darned if I know."

HALF AN HOUR later they managed to drag Ben to the tunnel opening. He neither helped nor resisted. Waiting above were Gage and three deputies, Micah Parish, Sarah Ironheart and Guy Redwing.

"Well, I'll be damned," Gage said.

Which pretty much said it all.

Chapter Sixteen

Two nights later, Candy stood inside the gymnasium, watching kids and teens romp, watching parents hand out generous amounts of candy.

Even though Ben Wittes was probably the killer, uneasiness still stalked the area. Besides, it was frigid outside, where the first huge flakes of winter had begun to fall in noticeable quantities. Tomorrow the entire world would be blanketed in a sparkling white coat.

Cleansing, Candy thought.

Steve, who'd come, as well, moved to her side. "Can you talk?"

"Sure." She nodded to Connie Parish, who nodded back. Connie would take over for a little while.

Outside, away from the door, their breath blew white clouds.

"I want to fill you in," he said. They hadn't seen each other since Ben Wittes's arrest.

"I'd like that."

"But I want some info in return."

She smiled into the icy air. "I figured. I can give you at least some."

"Thanks." He rocked on his feet a couple of times.

"The Castelles are torn between shock, horror and relief."

"I'd expect that."

"They want to fill in the tunnel. They're going to wait, though, until after we film."

She faced him, surprised. "They still want to do the show?"

"Yup. I'm amazed, too. But Annabelle and Todd said they want the truth out there. To tell people that not everything terrifying is a ghost."

"Um, wow." She thought about that. "But isn't this scarier? Really? Wouldn't it be better for people to worry about ghosts?"

"They don't think so, and neither do my producers. Psychologists will probably be thrilled to be dealing with something besides ghosts."

"Maybe. But what's more terrifying?"

"Not my decision. Consider how many TV shows deal with real murders. People watch them more than they watch ghosts. If that doesn't frighten them, this shouldn't."

He had a point. People were fascinated by true crime stories and didn't have nightmares about them. "Well, you're in line with your principles." Principles she now believed he had.

"Exactly. No lying to the audience. No pretending that something is real when it's not."

"How's Viv doing?"

"They're still promising her the mean man is gone, that he's been arrested by the police. I told her, too. It may take her a while."

Candy felt truly sorry for Vivian. She didn't deserve the terrors that would now probably follow her for a long time. "That's to be expected. That little girl has been scared for nearly a year. Unable to sleep in her own bedroom."

Steve nodded. Snowflakes had begun to collect on his knit cap. "Buddy seems to be relieved, too. No more sessions growling at the wall. I think his reaction is going to do more for Vivian than anything we tell her."

"It probably will."

He tilted his head. "Your turn."

"Well, it gets complicated. We found a sedative in Ben's trunk. The same one used on the teens. We also found clothes in his hamper that are covered with dirt and pine needles. Thing is, he claims not to remember any of it. Sadly, I think he's telling the truth."

"How could that be?" Steve sounded dubious.

"We can't detect any lying. Besides, the first time we mentioned the murders, before they became public knowledge, his face turned a ghastly white. Nobody could fake that drop in blood pressure."

"Unless he was a meditating Buddhist monk anyway. So he killed those kids."

"We've got enough evidence to hold him. We'll get the rest."

"And the body in the coffin?"

She sighed. "It's old. The medical examiner says a female, age around forty. She appears to have been killed in a fall down some stairs."

Steve rocked again on his feet. "So that Bride guy is cleared?"

"Maybe so. Ben is claiming that Sam told him to take care of her, to talk to her and sing to her. He keeps saying that Samuel Bride didn't kill her."

Steve didn't answer for a long time. "How can Ben

not remember the murders? And how can he be so sure that Bride didn't kill his wife?"

"I don't know. I really don't. We're beginning to believe there's something loose in his head."

"Maybe." Steve sighed. "Please get the answers. I really don't want to start wondering if that guy is truly psychic."

Despite the circumstances, Candy had to laugh. "I couldn't agree more."

Then Steve smiled at her. "You open for coffee after this shindig winds down?"

Her heart leaped. Oh, this was bad. She ought to tell him no, to start distancing herself. Instead she said, "Yes."

KIDS, STEVE THOUGHT. He got a kick out of watching the youngsters squeal their way through the haunted house that ran along a hallway that opened off the gym.

Candy told him the teens who worked on the party had toned it down so it wouldn't be too scary for the little ones.

And somebody had even found a copy of "Monster Mash" to play, which had kids of every age dancing all around the gym.

But when midnight came, parents had a difficult time trying to round up everyone. Steve remembered the days when he could stay up into the wee hours having a good time. Remembered. He couldn't do that easily anymore.

But at last Candy escaped and he followed her home, wondering if he should go by the truck stop to get coffee and a nibble for them. It would be nicer, he decided, than dumping all that on Candy at this hour.

She was waiting when he arrived, looking wide

awake. The evening must have stimulated her. For his part, sleepiness stalked the edges of his mind.

But he needed to spend time with her. Needed to talk with her. Hope was slender, but he had to try. Emotions were welling up in him, beyond his ability to control.

She curled up on her couch beneath a warm throw, sipping coffee and eating a jelly-filled doughnut. "I love these doughnuts," she remarked. "Ever since I was little. I didn't get them very often. My mama and my abuela—that's my grandmother—had a whole bunch of desserts they made, from flan to three-milk cake. Empanadas. All good. Excellent in fact. But not jelly doughnuts."

He hesitated, his own doughnut forgotten. "You don't talk much about your Latin heritage, do you?"

She sighed and shook her head. "It's not a popular topic. Besides, I took enough guff about it when I was in school. It was better in the Army."

Another sign of her growing trust for him. He felt honored. "I don't think you should have to hide it, Candy."

"Maybe I shouldn't have to, but life has taught me otherwise. You know, my family has been in California since it was a Spanish colony. People don't want to know that either. I was frequently told that I should go back to Mexico." She snorted. "My family was there, too, when the state was *part* of Mexico."

"People can be such ignoramuses."

"I doubt many of their school history classes covered the subject. I try to excuse it now, but back then it really hurt."

He didn't answer immediately, seeking the right words. But then there didn't seem to be any but the bald truth. "I've seen it. I've seen a lot of it, and it just seems to keep getting uglier. For indigenous peoples, too. Man, they've been here for at least twenty-five thousand years."

"The world is filled with conveniently short memories."

"Except yours," he said quietly.

Her head raised. "I need to apologize for that night."

"No, you don't. Not ever, not with me. End of discussion."

The jelly filling was gone from her doughnut. He watched her put it aside. "Hey, that's not a cop thing to do!"

She laughed. "Maybe not. How'd that get started anyway?"

"Cops work ridiculous hours and there aren't many places open in the middle of the night. Run in, grab a coffee and a doughnut, then get back on the road. Some places offer it for free."

She lifted a brow. "Isn't that a bribe?"

"No. They never asked anything in return. I always figured they just liked the traffic in their parking lots during those hours."

"Police protection?"

He shook his head. "Police presence for all of four minutes at a time. Like I said, they never asked for a thing, and a dollar cup of coffee and a fifty-cent doughnut hardly classify as a bribe."

"I wouldn't do anything in exchange for that."

"Exactly." He was having a terrible time coming around to what he most wanted to discuss with her. If his hand grew any tighter around his cup of coffee, he was going to crush it.

"Candy?"

"Yeah?" She appeared to have drifted away a little.

"Am I right in thinking you don't want to go back to California?"

"Maybe for a visit eventually. But to stay? I like it a whole lot better here."

"I thought so. So I want to make a proposition."

He had her full attention now. Putting his coffee down, he crossed to sit beside her curled-up legs on the couch. "How would you feel if I came back to visit *you*?"

CANDY CAUGHT HER BREATH. Every cell in her being seemed to be reaching out toward Steve, but she held still. Where was this going? "I wouldn't mind."

"Good." He paused, keeping her dangling somewhere near hope, but also near fear.

God, what was he suggesting?"

"Thing is," he said slowly, "I wasn't kidding when I said I want to know you better. I wasn't kidding when I said I want you. Damn me for a boor if you want."

Her heart was tripping fast now. Heat began to sizzle throughout her body. "You're not a boor."

He compressed his lips for a few seconds, then spoke again. "What I want is a relationship. Hell, I want more than that, but you must need time. But if we build something bigger, it's okay if you don't want to move to California."

Now she could barely breathe. "Why not?"

"My home is there, but I'm almost never there anyway. I could come visit you between programs, between seasons. You don't need to live with me in an empty house for long stretches. Without the job you clearly love, or the friends you're making here."

Now there didn't seem to be any air left in the universe. Her heart and mind had caught on one thing. Live with him? "Steve?"

"I'm a bumbling fool. What I'm trying to say is that I've fallen in love with you, and if you eventually see your way to feeling the same about me, then we can make it work."

It was such a huge prospect that she had trouble absorbing it. A life she'd given up hoping for was now offering her the possibility of it becoming true?

But he'd stayed with her an entire night after her meltdown. He'd never criticized her for it. Instead he'd offered understanding and comfort. Now he wanted to offer her more.

Truth and reality both began to dawn on her, and as they did her heart soared. Honesty caused her to blurt a fact she'd been hiding from herself. "I think I love you, too."

The biggest smile spread across his face. "You've just made me the happiest man alive."

Then, leaning over, he scooped her up into his arms. "Now for the other part of what I want. If you don't mind."

The heat inside her became electric. "Why would I mind? I want you, too."

Then he carried her off to her bed, the first steps on a road to a new future.

She knew she could handle this. She knew she was going to love every minute.

A new day was creeping into the world, and into her heart.

* * * * *

*Don't miss other romances in Rachel Lee's thrilling
Conard County: The Next Generation series:*

Available now from Harlequin Books

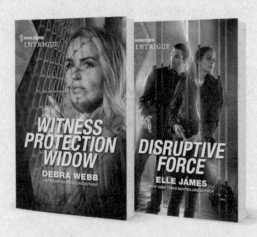

COMING NEXT MONTH FROM

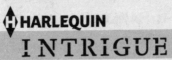

HARLEQUIN
INTRIGUE

Available September 15, 2020

#1953 SUSPICIOUS CIRCUMSTANCES
A Badge of Honor Mystery • by Rita Herron
Special agent Liam Maverick asks for nurse Peyton Weiss's help in his hunt for the person who caused the hospital fire that killed his father. But someone doesn't want Peyton to share what she knows...and they'll do whatever it takes to keep her quiet.

#1954 TEXAS KIDNAPPING
An O'Connor Family Mystery • by Barb Han
After stopping a would-be kidnapper from taking her newly adopted daughter, Renee Smith accepts US Marshal Cash O'Connor's offer of a safe haven at his Texas ranch. The case resembles his sister's unsolved kidnapping thirty years ago, and Cash won't allow history to repeat itself.

#1955 THE LINE OF DUTY
Blackhawk Security • by Nichole Severn
When Blackhawk operative Vincent Kalani boarded an airplane, he never expected it to crash into the Alaskan mountains, but by-the-book police officer Shea Ramsey soon becomes his unlikely partner in survival. Can they escape the wilderness, or will their attackers find them first?

#1956 MARINE PROTECTOR
Fortress Defense • by Julie Anne Lindsey
Pursued by a madman, single mom Lyndy Wells and her infant son are bodyguard Cade Lance's priority assignment. Cade knows they must find the serial killer quickly or Lyndy and her baby will face grave danger. And Cade won't let that happen on his watch.

#1957 WITNESS SECURITY BREACH
A Hard Core Justice Thriller • by Juno Rushdan
There's not a target out there that US Marshals Aiden Yazzie and Charlotte "Charlie" Killinger can't bring down. Until a high-profile witness goes missing and a fellow marshal is murdered? Can they steer clear of temptation to find their witness before it's too late?

#1958 STALKED IN THE NIGHT
by Carla Cassidy
The target of a brutal criminal, Eva Martin is determined to defend her son and her ranch. Jake Albright is a complication she doesn't need—especially since he doesn't know about their child. As danger escalates and a shared desire grows, can Eva hold on to the family she's just regained?

HICNM0920

He had a lead.

The partial fingerprint he'd lifted from the murder
scene hadn't been a partial at all, but evidence of a severe
burn on the owner's index finger that altered the print.
He hadn't been able to get an ID with so few markers to
compare before leaving New York City a year ago. But
now, Blackhawk Security forensic expert Vincent Kalani
finally had a chance to bring down a killer.

He hauled his duffel bag higher on his shoulder.
He had to get back to New York, convince his former
commanding officer to reopen the case. His muscles
burned under the weight as he ducked beneath the small
passenger plane's wing and climbed inside. Cold Alaskan
air drove beneath his heavy coat, but catching sight of the
second passenger already aboard chased back the chill.

"Shea Ramsey." Long, curly dark hair slid over her shoulder as jade-green eyes widened in surprise. His entire body nearly gave in to the increased sense of gravity pulling at him had it not been for the paralysis working through his muscles. Officer Shea Ramsey had assisted Blackhawk Security with investigations in the past at the insistence of Anchorage's chief of police, but her form-fitting pair of jeans, T-shirt and zip-up hoodie announced she wasn't here on business. Hell, she was a damn beautiful woman, an even better investigator and apparently headed to New York. Same as him. "Anchorage Police Department's finest, indeed."

"What the hell are you doing here?" Shea shuffled her small backpack at her feet, crossing her arms over her midsection. The tendons between her shoulders and neck corded with tension as she stared out her side of the plane. No mistaking the bitterness in her voice. "Is Blackhawk following me now?"

"Should we be?"

Don't miss
The Line of Duty *by Nichole Severn,*
available October 2020 wherever
Harlequin Intrigue books and ebooks are sold.

Harlequin.com

HIEXP0920